'Don't look so glum, Doctor.'

'Nobody expects you to know everything about the town from the word go.'

'I should hope not,' Jenna answered tightly. 'And, that being so, perhaps a little less one-upmanship every time I show my ignorance would be—charitable.'

Rob drew in his breath with an audible hiss, but Jenna didn't wait for the crushing reply he'd be sure to make.

Dear Reader

This month we touch upon personal grief for the heroines in TROUBLED HEARTS by Christine Adams, and SUNLIGHT AND SHADOW by Frances Crowne, both handled with sensitivity. PARTNERS IN PRIDE by Drusilla Douglas and A TESTING TIME (set in Australia) by Meredith Webber give us heroines who are trying hard to make a fresh start in life, not always an easy thing to do—we think you'll both laugh and cry.

The Editor

Drusilla Douglas is a physiotherapist who has written numerous short stories—mainly for Scottish based magazines. Now the luxury of working part-time has provided her with the leisure necessary for writing novels.

Recent titles by the same author:

A BORDER PRACTICE
SURGEON'S STRATEGY

PARTNERS IN PRIDE

BY
DRUSILLA DOUGLAS

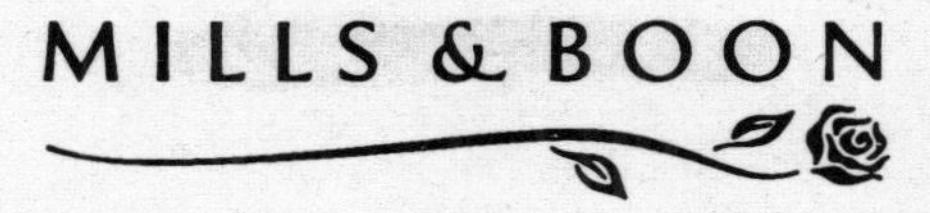

MILLS & BOON LIMITED
ETON HOUSE, 18–24 PARADISE ROAD
RICHMOND, SURREY, TW9 1SR

All the characters in this book have no existence outside the imagination of the Author, and have no relation whatsoever to anyone bearing the same name or names. They are not even distantly inspired by any individual known or unknown to the Author, and all the incidents are pure invention.

First published in Great Britain 1994
by Mills & Boon Limited

ISBN 0 263 13985 9

Set in 10 on 11½ pt Linotron Times
15-9404-55815

Typeset in Great Britain by Centracet, Cambridge
Made and printed in Great Britain

CHAPTER ONE

DR JENNA FIELDING was regretting her decision even before she paid the toll at the Forth Road Bridge. The rolling fields of Fife and lower Tayside did nothing to lighten her mood. And by the time she caught her first glimpse of the North Sea—stormy, dark and coldly threatening—she was wondering if she'd flipped. It wasn't necessary to have put so many miles between herself and Jake. Fifty, and that practice in the pretty little Perthshire town with the name she couldn't pronounce, would have done. But no. The deplorably masochistic streak that had prompted her to follow him from Leeds to Edinburgh when he beckoned had nudged her again into this. Flight—after the final souring of their relationship.

It hadn't been difficult to arrange. Nobody else on the GP training course had wanted this remote posting. Why would they? Jenna asked herself despairingly as she stopped the car and got out for a closer look at the drab grey buildings of Port Lindsay, huddled together all anyhow at the foot of the cliff. A sudden squall swept inland, stopping her breath in its icy spite. Jenna ran back to her car and restarted the engine.

From the main highway it hadn't been possible to see the sturdy detached Victorian villas flanking the long road which wound gently downhill to sea level. She hadn't expected anything this prosperous, so perhaps the little fishing town of Port Lindsay wasn't quite the backwater she'd supposed. Lower down, though, the houses were smaller and had dwindled to terraced cottages by the time she spied the water front.

Shore Street, where the surgery was, enclosed a large double harbour in a near-perfect horseshoe shape. About twenty small fishing trawlers were tied up there and piles of fishing gear lay in untidy heaps on the quayside. There was a surprising amount of traffic so, rather than drive up and down looking for Harbour House, Jenna parked outside the Seamen's Mission and went in to ask for directions.

A seabooted man in typical sweater and woolly cap removed a pipe from his mouth to puff out a cloud of pungent tabacco smoke and ask,'Is it the doctors' place you're wantin'?' When Jenna nodded, he told her, 'It's aboot halfway along the north side, but evening surgery's not till the back o' five.' He was looking her over with open curiosity. 'Ye're new to the town,' he stated.

Jenna smiled, confirmed that, thanked him politely for his help and left, followed by a wave of curious glances.

Harbour House was surprisingly large: double-fronted and three storeys high, not counting the attics. A door to the right bore the simple statement—'SURGERY. Drs W. & R. Strachan.' But, mindful of her information, Jenna climbed the three steep steps from the pavement and rang the front doorbell. She rang several times before giving up and retreating to the car. It was raining hard and she was soaked. What an arrival! And she'd told them almost to the minute what time she'd be here. She had quite decided she wasn't going to like the Drs Strachan one bit, when the front door opened and a tall, gaunt woman looked out, peering to right and left. She had the door half shut again before Jenna had got out, dodged round a man with an armful of oilskins, and rushed back calling frantically, 'No, wait—please! I'm Dr Fielding.'

She found herself on the receiving end of very cool appraisal.

'You're very young,' said the woman. She was blocking the doorway, keeping Jenna out in the rain.

'I'm older than I look, Mrs—Strachan?'

'There is no Mrs Strachan—now. I'm Mrs Cullen, the housekeeper.'

'How do you do, Mrs Cullen,' Jenna said politely. 'May I come in, please? I'm getting very wet.'

'Aye, it's that sort of day.' She stood aside at last, allowing Jenna into the hall. 'Have ye no luggage?' she asked then, suspiciously.

What a silly question, when Jenna was here for three months mimimum and a year if things turned out to mutual satisfaction. 'It seemed sensible to leave it in the car until it stops raining.'

'Aye,' said Mrs Cullen once more.

'But now, having got so *very* wet, I need to change and——' Jenna sneezed violently. 'And perhaps a bath?'

'I daresay that'd be all right.' She didn't sound very sure. 'I'll go and find ye a towel.'

'While I bring in as much as I need,' decided Jenna. 'Please don't lock me out.'

'I take it the doctors are out on their rounds,' she said to the housekeeper when she'd staggered back into the house with her two largest cases.

'Aye, they are—though they'll likely be in shortly for their tea. Your room's the door on the right on the first floor and the bathroom's the door on the half landing. Can ye manage?'

Since she was presumably referring to her luggage and not questioning the new assistant's ability to scrub her own back, Jenna took the wind out her sails saying how wonderfully kind; her car was the red VW Polo outside the ship's chandlers and here were the keys. Then she humped her cases up the stairs.

The bathroom was amazing. Jenna doubted it had been altered since the day it was put in, pre-First World War. The bolt on the door was certainly an original and obviously no longer up to its job. For want of better protection, Jenna wedged a chair under the door knob and prepared to enjoy a good wallow in the massive tub. The water was piping hot and unexpectedly soft, so half the amount of bath essence would have done. Never mind —she'd know better next time. She sank thankfully into her sea of foam and closed her eyes.

Last night's parting with Jake had been every bit a traumatic as she'd feared. He'd been persuasive and petulant by turns—just the way he always was when he thought she was getting away from him—giving her a wakeful night as a result. So what with shortage of sleep and the soothing effect of the hot water, Jenna was dozing when the door was flung open with an energy that sent the chair toppling sideways with a mighty crash.

She bounced up, realised a man was standing dumbstruck in the doorway, gave a maidenly shriek and folded her arms across her breasts. 'How dare you?' she snarled when he went on staring. 'Get out this minute, you—you. . .!'

He came out of his trance at that, but continued to stand there, feet apart and arms folded. 'Dr Fielding, I presume,' he drawled in a beguiling baritone, at variance with his rugged features and mocking, deep-set blue eyes. 'I'm Robert Strachan. And there's no need to blush. You're more than adequately concealed by all that foam.'

'And a very good thing too, when the bolt on that door is absolutely useless!' snapped Jenna with great presence of mind. God! If his medicine was as antiquated as his household gadgets, then——

But he was silently demonstrating how easy it was to secure the door by rotating a tiny button in the middle of the doorknob.

'Oh!' breathed Jenna, furious with herself for not discovering that.

Dr Robert Strachan smiled smugly, infuriating her some more. 'Well, don't blame me for not noticing,' she fumed. 'Who would expect anything so modern in—in a——'

'Museum?' he asked with devastating intuition. 'We're canny folk up here, Dr Fielding, and we don't fling our money at every new fashion. If something works well—like that bathtub you are filling so charmingly—then we keep it. But when something gives out—like this bolt—we replace it with the best thing for the job. Tea in the sitting-room in about fifteen minutes.'

Before Jenna could retaliate, he had shut the door and was running downstairs, whistling.

She continued to fume and glare at the space where he'd been. She'd made some inauspicious starts in her time, but nothing quite as bad as this. First that battleaxe of a housekeeper and now him. And the fact that Dr Robert Strachan, though not the most handsome, was certainly as interesting and masculine a man as she'd met in a very long time only made it worse. If the father's anything like the son, then I'm going back to Edinburgh tomorrow, she resolved grimly as she stood up to flick the foam off her slender body before reaching for the towel.

She put on clean undies and the first sweater and skirt she unearthed. Then she refastened her cases and went to find her room. It was a very pleasant surprise: well carpeted, spacious and the depth of the house, with two long windows to the front, overlooking the harbour, and another to the rear. However, in view of Dr Strachan's fifteen-minute warning, she only stayed long enough to put a brush through her thick blonde hair and take the shine off her nose before hurrying downstairs.

In the sitting-room, a grey-haired man in his early sixties was piling logs on the fire. When he heard Jenna come in, he clapped a hand to his back and straightened up with some difficulty. 'Rheumatism—the scourge of advancing years,' he explained, coming forward to greet her, hand outstretched. 'William Strachan. Welcome to Port Lindsay, Dr Fielding.'

'Jenna, please,' she said, liking him on sight. His blue eyes, less vivid than his son's, were calm and clear, engendering instant trust.

He led her to a massive couch on one side of the blazing fire. A laden tea tray filled the low table in front of it. 'We'll not wait for Rob,' he said, picking up the teapot. 'A call came in soon after he got back and there's no telling how long he'll be. Milk and sugar?'

'Just milk, please. Doctor. Do you make many home visits, then?' she asked, anxious to find out all she could before Dr Strachan junior returned. She had this feeling that he would be a harder task-master than his gentle father.

Dr William looked faintly surprised at her question. 'As many as are needed,' he returned, confirming her instinctive belief that, with him, the patients would come first. 'I've read the circulars, of course,' he continued when he'd finished his scone. 'Get 'em all to come to the surgery and save money seems to be the current thinking, but to my mind it's a pity they ever started all this costing and meddling. Pay a doctor adequately and only rap him over the knuckles if he doesn't do a good job. That's my philosophy,'

'But some patients do call us out unnecessarily, don't they, Doctor? At least that's what we were told on the course. . .'

'Aye, they do, lassie—and then I give them a richt guid telling. But better that than have some puir wee body struggling out and collapsing in the street. Rob agrees with me,' he wound up.

Which could be why he'd gone out when he did, instead of having his tea first, supposed Jenna, just as the door opened and the man himself came in.

Raindrops glistened on his untidy thatch of brown hair and the wind had given an extra glow to his already healthy tan. He dropped easily into the chair opposite, stretching his long legs towards the blaze and folding his hands behind his head. A wry grin enlivened his rugged features as he told his father, 'The Browns again. Wee Geordie decided to try his hand at the mincer. Literally. Fortunately, it's a very old mincer and little damage was done.'

Jenna thought that definitely sounded like a unnecessary home visit. 'Couldn't one of his parents have brought him to evening surgery?' she asked impulsively.

The vivid blue eyes searched her face, their expression faintly mocking. 'Wee Geordie is the third of five—all under the age of eight,' he began. 'His mother is very frail and not very bright. As for his father, nobody knows where or even who he is.'

'So not all problem families live in urban slums, then,' exclaimed Jenna, appalled. Common sense suggested that she left it there, but recent lectures were too vivid in her mind. 'Wouldn't all those children be better off in care, if the mother isn't coping?' she asked.

'Did I say she wasn't coping?' asked Dr Strachan junior. 'She looks after them remarkably well, all things considered, and I've seen less motherly concern in douce city villas.' He didn't tell her where.

'But five. . .and presumably she'll have more!' By the next passing stranger, no doubt. What a mess some women made of their lives.

'Not very likely. The last one all but finished her off, the puir soul. You'll learn,' said Rob Strachan with infuriating superiority as he leaned forward to pour himself some tea. 'When to meddle and when to leave well alone,' he added in case Jenna hadn't taken his point.

She would have liked to defend her position but was only too well aware that she'd brought that reproof on herself by asking a rash question in the first place. Sit tight and observe carefully before questioning what you see and hear had been good advice given to trainee GPs—and she hadn't done that. 'Um, nothing's ever—well, black and white, is it? she mumbled.

'No, unfortunately,' agreed her mentor through a mouthful of wonderful-looking fruit cake. 'Jeannie's surpassed herself this time,' he told his father. 'Have a slice, Dr Fielding.'

'No, thank you. I don't usually eat anything at this time——' Now he'd think she was either on a diet or reproving him for over indulgence.

'Suit yourself,' he shrugged, 'but you'll be sorry. It's

a marathon surgery tonight and there's no telling what time you'll get your supper.'

Jenna took that to mean that she'd be taking surgery by herself and she couldn't help feeling rather resentful. 'Perhaps I should go through now, then, and—and acquaint myself with the layout,' she said shortly.

'All in good time,' replied Rob Strachan. 'I've not finished my tea yet.'

'I wouldn't wish to put you to any trouble, Doctor.'

'And I don't imagine you will—*Doctor*—but unless you're psychic, you'll need some guidance.'

So he'd seen her gesture as a bid for independence, then. If I don't learn to put things in a way he can't possibly misunderstand, I could be in for trouble, Jenna realised.

Evening surgery was at five-thirty, and at five twenty-three, Rob Strachan got to his feet, stretched his arms sideways and then led Jenna out of the room, across the hall and into the dining-room, where he opened a door beside the fireplace. It gave on to a narrow windowless passage. A murmur of voices at the end suggested the waiting-room, but before they got that far Rob opened the door of a consulting room.

Jenna gazed round in amazement. 'Right out of the pages of Dr Finlay?' he queried, reading her reaction aright. Why couldn't he do that when it really mattered?

'I think it's—very civilised,' she returned, referring to the heavy old-fashioned desk, the swivel oak chair and the two-tier glass-fronted bookcase stuffed with textbooks. There was even a square of good carpet on the floor. It might have been a lawyer's office, until one spotted the examination couch, gleaming worktop and modern instrument trolley.

'Will it do?' Rob asked satirically.

'The facilities are excellent,' Jenna returned quietly. 'Is the other room the same?'

'There isn't one,' he said, enjoying her surprise.

So she'd not been wrong to assume she'd be doing this surgery alone. 'I see,' she said slowly. 'Well, thank you very much for showing me this much, Doctor. Now I'd better get started.

'Not without this,' he said, taking a freshly starched white coat from a cupboard and tossing it across to her. He donned a second one himself, after placing another chair behind the desk. Then he picked up the first folder from a big pile of notes and went along the passage to call in the first patient. Jenna wondered why they didn't have a receptionist, but resolved to keep that question for Dr Strachan senior, who'd be less likely to take it for criticism!

Jenna soon found that her role was that of observer, and, as she'd expected of an evening surgery, most of the patients were working folk with a succession of minor aches and pains, or work-related injuries. What came across most clearly was the knowledge Rob Strachan had of them all. Friendly enquiries about families and hobbies intermingled with professional questions and advice. To one whose working life had so far been spent in hospitals, it was a revelation. But then presumably he had grown up in Port Lindsay, gaining invaluable glimpses into the lives of his future patients in the process.

'What are your impressions so far?' he asked while they waited for the last patient.

'Knowing the patient's background is a tremendous advantage,' she returned promptly.

'In some ways, yes. On the other hand, knowing folk too well can make it harder to keep a professional distance.'

'I can see that too — though you seem to manage it.'

'I'm flattered,' he said without sounding it. 'Now I wonder what you'll make of our last one,' he murmered as a small, miserable-looking woman shuffled in and took the patient's chair.

'Well now, Wilma, and how are you today?' asked Rob, having introduced his new colleague from Edinburgh.

'I'm worse,' said the patient.

'In what way?' he asked gently.

'Every which way,' she answered without clarifying things.

'Pain, nausea, dizziness. . .'

'The headache's back this week, Dr Rob. Sometimes I think it'll split in two. Are ye quite sure it's no' a tumour?'

From the careful way he explained that the scan, the X-rays and all the other tests were negative, Jenna gathered that this was an exchange they'd often had before.

'So why the pain, then?' asked the patient, unconvinced.

'Pain isn't always a symptom. Sometimes it's a condition in itself,' said Rob in the same gentle way. 'That's why I'm going to start you on some new pills.'

Glancing sideways, Jenna saw that he was writing a prescription for the latest thing in anti-depressants.

'But will they cure the pain?' asked the patient.

'More than likely,' he returned carefully. 'And they'll certainly make you feel a lot better in yourself.'

'A tonic, like, then.'

'In a way. Did you go to the Church coffee morning as I suggested?'

'I did not. I wasn't up to it — and besides, they're a

gey snooty lot who run it. Any road, I prefer keeping myself to myself, ye ken.'

'I know you do, Wilma, but it'd do you good to get out and mix more.'

'My health does not allow me to go gadding about,' she reproved him.

They were going round in circles and he knew it. 'But once these new pills take effect, you'll be a different woman,' he said in a persuasive tone that would have convinced anybody else.

'I'll come back next week and let you know,' said the woman doggedly.

'Give it two weeks, Wilma. They need time to work.'

'Are you telling me that I cannae come and see ye for a fortnight no matter how bad I feel?'

'Of course not—just warning you not to expect an overnight miracle. The change of medicine will do you a lot of good in the long run though.'

'We'll see,' said Miss Wilma Smith. 'We'll see. Now this will have to do for today, or the chippie will be shut and I'll not get ma supper. I think mebbe I should have an afternoon appointment next week. I was hearing you don't rush folk so much in the afternoons.'

With great presence of mind he said, 'I'll be asking Meg to send you a card. There'll be some changes in the routine, now that there are three of us.' He got to his feet and shepherded her out of the room, asking, 'Did you get the council to fix that window that was bothering you?'

'Fix, did ye say. . .?' Jenna listened to the complaining voice growing fainter as they went down the passage, before leaning over to flick through the patient's notes. It certainly seemed as though she'd been thoroughly investigated, but she was remembering a similar case. . .

'I encountered a patient just like Miss Smith in the Royal Infirmary in Edinburgh last year,' she said as soon as Rob appeared. 'She'd been passed from doctor to doctor for years. When she eventually came to us in neurosurgery, she had an inoperable tumour.'

He perched on the corner of the desk and looked down on her with barely concealed impatience. 'I believe you,' he said at last, 'but it's quite certain that Wilma Smith doesn't have anything sinister at present. However, these unhappy people are as likely as anybody else to develop something organic and unpleasant—which is why her complaints will never be glossed over in *this* practice.' He hung up his white coat. 'If, as I feel sure you did, you've looked at her notes, you'll see we have her down as a severe depressive personality disorder. Now if you have any useful comments about that, I'll be glad to hear them. To my mind, that's one of the most tragic of health problems, when it effectively prevents the formation of close personal relationships.'

Jenna was scarlet by then. 'Well—off hand, no, I can't——'

'Good,' he cut in decisively. 'Now let's go and eat. In case you haven't noticed, it's now well after eight.'

'Is it really? The time passed so quickly. . .' She paused, conscious that the right comment on the session could lessen his annoyance. 'That was all very instructive, thank you, Doctor,' she offered.

'What! A succession of aches and bruises and one unhappy loner?' he simplified. 'You amaze me.'

And *you're* rapidly making *me* very cross. . . 'All the same, I really feel I've learned something,' Jenna persisted doggedly. 'Not least, how to put patients at their ease. I'd never suspected that—that. . .' She stuttered to a stop. What she'd almost said would have set back the cause of harmony to the point of no return! What a blessing that Dr William came in just then, to tell them that supper was on the table. 'We only use the dining-room on state occasions, my dear,' he explained to Jenna, 'so come away through to the kitchen. You must be starving.'

'One thing I'm already sure of is that nobody is likely to starve in this house,' she returned with a smile.

The kitchen was warm, modern and well-equipped—another instance of replacing with the best when the old gave out?

A round pine table was set for three, so the disapproving Mrs Cullen wouldn't be sitting down with them. Her cottage pie and apple crumble were as good as her teatime scones and cakes, and Jenna wondered how long she'd keep her waistline if this went on.

'No, really, I couldn't eat another morsel,' she insisted when Dr William said what a shame it was to leave such a little bit of pudding. 'I never eat puddings as a rule,' she added.

'Oh, lord, not another dieter,' Dr Rob sighed gloomily, getting up to pour coffee from the pot keeping warm on the Aga.

Peaceable as ever, his father said there was a world of difference between their last trainee's insistence on organically grown salads with everything, and a slip of a girl not being able to keep up with two men in the consumption stakes, but Rob wasn't consoled.

Jenna had already worked out that her predecessor was female, so was Rob Strachan anti-women doctors then? Very likely, when chauvinism was alive and well in so many aspects of medical practice. Sweetly, she asked him to pass the sugar and ladled two generous spoonfuls into her cup, stirring thoroughly under his cynical gaze. 'I have a very sweet tooth,' she found herself explaining defensively.

Rob cocked a derisive eyebrow. 'Really? You could have fooled me.'

'I do try to—to keep it under control. . .' What's the matter with me? she thought. Why can't I behave like the poised professional woman I am? Well, most of the time anyway!

'Yes, one should always try to control excessive self-indulgence,' returned Rob Strachan to Jenna's fury. That wasn't what she'd meant at all. Another instance of misunderstanding or was he deliberately trying to provoke her?

Dr William who'd been looking and listening as if he didn't know what to make of it, then said firmly that he for one now intended to be very self-indulgent and get away to his bed. 'I've had a busy day,' he added in self-defence.

'There weren't any calls during surgery, I hope,' his son put in quickly.

'No, no, my boy—I've not been out of the house since teatime.' He turned to Jenna and held out his hand. 'I hope you'll be comfortable and very happy while you're here with us, Dr Jenna,' he said simply before wishing them both goodnight and shuffling out of the room.

His son watched his exit with a worried frown. 'My father is not a well man,' he said.

'I had wondered,' confessed Jenna. 'I mean, apart from his generalised osteo-arthrosis——' She bit her lip. She'd done it again—jumping to conclusions. And about the senior partner too.

Rob didn't react unfavourably this time though. 'You've noticed his colour,' he assumed.

She admitted as much.

'He contracted acute infective hepatitis about six months ago. There was an outbreak at a travellers' encampment, and he was unlucky. It followed the usual course and I'm hopeful there's no permanent liver damage, but he's taking longer that I'd like to regain his energy. I try to stop him overdoing things, but it's not easy. He lives for his work since my mother died.'

And what do you live for, Dr Robert? Jenna found herself wondering, but what she said was, 'Yes, losing one's spouse must be a terrible thing.'

'Not invariably,' he disagreed. 'Sometimes, it's a blessed relief.' He had spoken with feeling, but when she looked at him questioningly he added, 'Not all marriages are made in heaven—as every doctor knows.'

'What I really meant was that to lose one's partner after a long and happy time together must be a terrible thing.'

'But that's not what you said the first time,' he reminded her.

'I can see I'm going to have to watch my words very carefully with you, Dr Strachan,' said Jenna, while determining that it was high time they got on to something more straightforward. 'Would Mrs Cullen be offended or pleased if I were to clear away and wash up?' she asked, getting up from the table.

'There's a dishwasher,' he told her, getting up too and dwarfing her slight five feet four. 'Go to bed, Dr Fielding,' he ordered. 'You must be tired.'

Very thoughtful, if I weren't so sure you just want me out of the way. 'I've done nothing all day, except drive up from Edinburgh, and the roads were very quiet.'

'All right, so you're not tired, but have you unpacked yet?'

Jenna shook her head.

'Then I suggest you do.'

This time she said aloud, 'You're most thoughtful, Doctor. I think I'm going to like working here.'

'It's to be hoped so,' he returned, lifting an eyebrow. 'A year is a long time to be unhappy in one's work.' He started to clear the table. 'Breakfast is at eight. And tomorrow you'll be going out with my father on his rounds.'

While he did surgery again. 'When will I actually be starting work, then?'

'As soon as you've got used to the set-up.'

Or did he mean as soon as he'd decided she was competent? 'I hadn't expected quite so much consideration, Doctor,' she said with gentle irony.

'Then you haven't read the recommendations to GPs, regarding trainee assistants,' he returned evenly. 'Goodnight, Dr Fielding. Sleep well.' Jenna was dismissed.

'Goodnight, Dr Strachan, she said quietly. 'And thank you.'

Jenna left the kitchen and started up the stairs. What *was* it about the man? It couldn't all be down to embarrassment at being caught in the bath. She hadn't felt this inadequate since her first year at medical school. And why in the world had she felt it necessary to thank him just now?

But Jenna shelved her perplexity when she opened the door of her room and looked round, viewing it properly this time. It had, she supposed, once been the drawing-room of the house, The front section was a comfortable sitting area, chintzy, cosy and charming. There was even a portable television set on a low table beside the fireplace. Beyond the archway, the smaller rear portion of the room held a single divan, a built-in wardrobe, a massive Victorian chest of drawers and a neat vanity unit. There was even a corner shower, and a telephone extension on the bedside table.

A far cry from the spartan quarters Jake had tried to depress her by describing when warning her what to expect in the frozen north-east, as he had called it. She'd really enjoy describing her lovely room to him when she wrote. Except that she wasn't going to write. Not this time. His latest tawdry little affair had been the final straw. As usual, he'd sworn to reform, but he'd broken that promise once too often. All that stuff about her being—deep down—the one and only! There was only so much hurt and humiliation a girl could take.

But she shouldn't be standing here, mooning and repining. She opened her cases and began putting things away. There were plenty of hangers in the massive wardrobe and more than enough space in the chest of drawers. But then she'd never been the type to go in for a vast array of clothes.

The bed was just as comfortable as she'd expected. Not that she would sleep much; did one ever on the first night in a strange place? And the strangest—no, the most intriguing thing about this particular place, was Dr Robert Strachan. . .

CHAPTER TWO

JENNA was awakened by a Schubert Serenade. She struggled into consciousness, both beguiled and bewildered. What on earth. . .? She reached out automatically to switch on her bedside light where it ought to be and scraped her knuckles on a wall. Puzzled, she turned over and saw the illuminated clock radio which had roused her. Then it all came back. But who would have thought she'd sleep so well?

It was half-past seven and Dr Rob had said that they breakfasted at eight. Loads of time, then. Jenna took a quick shower before dressing in a simple navy blue suit and plain white blouse for her first day as a GP. She kept her make-up to a minimum and tied back her blonde hair with a dark ribbon.

'Good lord!' exclaimed Rob Strachan, looking up from his porridge when she entered the kitchen. His shirt was open at the neck and his rolled-up sleeves showed off his strong bronzed forearms. Jenna wondered if he would be putting on a tie before surgery.

'Good morning, Doctor,' she said. She'd meant to sound polite, not disapproving.

He got unhurriedly to his feet and lounged over to the stove.

'You'll take some porridge,' he assumed.

'No, thanks, I'd rather——' But there probably wasn't any muesli in the house. 'I never eat much breakfast.'

'That's not very sensible,' he remarked in the tone and words she'd heard him use to more than one misguided patient the night before. 'And hardly worth sitting down for. Try this.' He put a steaming bowl down in front of her. 'Highly nutritious and not at all fattening. Unless of course your sweet tooth makes you ruin it with sugar.'

Jenna eyed him with flashing green eyes. You're a bully, said her glance, but she wasn't going to quarrel with him this early in the day. She tipped milk over the disgusting-looking stuff in the bowl and risked a tiny spoonful, but the milk was cream and the porridge as smooth as silk and absolutely delicious.

'Tea or coffee?' asked Dr Rob.

'You mean I'm allowed to choose?' Jenna asked, wide-eyed.

He sensed the irony. With an answering gleam he said, 'Only because my father and I differ about the best way of taking our morning dose of caffeine.'

'I'll wait a while—if I may,' she decided. When his father appeared, she'd take what he did.

'I get it,' he said, grinning as he poured himself some coffee.

So intuitive! Why hadn't he shown similar insight when they talked shop last evening?

Mrs Cullen bustled in from the utility room, hoped quite nicely that Jenna had slept well, took away her empty bowl and replaced it with a dainty helping of scrambled egg on toast. Then, in a much warmer way, she fussed Dr William into his seat when he appeared.

The scrambled egg was perfect and Jenna had eaten it all before she remembered claiming not to each much breakfast. 'It must be the sea air,' she supposed in answer to Dr Rob's satirical look.

Unaware of any undercurrents, Dr William began outlining his plans for her day. 'And then it'll be back here for lunch, Jenna, after which you can sit in with Rob this afternoon,' he concluded.

'Three surgeries a day, then,' she calculated. They certainly gave a good service, these two.

'Not exactly,' Rob contradicted. 'Afternoons are when we see any knotty problems turning up in surgery and requiring more than a cursory examination.'

'I'm impressed,' said Jenna, meaning that. And then, 'Coffee, please,' she said unguardedly when Dr William asked what she was drinking.

'So we actually have something in common after all,' said Rob in a honeyed voice. 'Now how about a warm roll?'

'Why not?' she sighed. 'I may as well have my entire calorific intake for the day at one go.' She split the roll and piled it high with butter and marmalade, while wondering if Port Lindsay was with-it enough to run to an aerobics class.

In the surgery, a capable looking woman in her late thirties was waiting to hand Dr William his list of visits. He introduced her to Jenna as, 'Meg Petrie, our long-time receptionist without whom we'd get into a terrible muddle.' A subsequent exchange about Meg's mother, currently a patient in the district hospital thirty miles away, explained her absence the night before. But for the senior partner's skilful intervention, Meg would have given Jenna a blow-by-blow account of her constant journeyings back and forth. I must study his technique, thought Jenna. It could come in very handy for dealing with over-chatty patients.

Jenna didn't think he was looking too well that morning, so she offered to take her car. 'Just an idea,' she added tactfully, 'but if you don't mind directing me, I think I'd learn my way about quicker if I did the driving.' He accepted her offer at face value and they set off.

Their first call was to a tiny cottage on the other side of the harbour; one of several, all white-washed and pantiled, with tiny deep-set windows and quaint outside stairs. 'Living quarters above and all the fishing gear stacked away below,' explained Jenna's mentor, 'although most of them are holiday cottages now, while the fisherfolk live much more comfortably in the new council houses behind the town.' He knocked on the weathered door before walking in with a cheery, 'Only me, Rosie. So what's this I'm hearing about a wee bit cold?'

An old lady draped in shawls was sitting up in a box bed in the kitchen. This was something Jenna had heard of, but not yet seen. She thought it must be like sleeping in a cupboard. 'Who's the wee lassie?' asked the patient. Dr William introduced his new assistant. 'A doctor, ye say?' queried Rosie. 'She looks as though she should still be at the school.'

That wasn't the first time such remarks had come Jenna's way and she wished she'd put on the plain specs she'd bought some time back as an ageing device. Dr William smiled as he took his stethoscope from his battered black bag and fought his way through the tangle of shawls to listen to Rosie's chest. He was very thorough about it. Then he took her pulse, squinted down her throat and looked to see if her ankles were swollen.

'All this to-do for a wee bit cold,' grumbled the old lady.

'Your wee bit cold is a touch of broncho-pneumonia,' said Dr William. 'And I'll be leaving a prescription for antibiotics at the chemist's. He'll send the girl along with it when they've got a minute. Now listen carefully.

You may get up if you keep to this nice warm room—it's better for your chest than staying in your bed—but there's no going out until I give the word. There's a snell wind blowing off the sea these last few days. Are you needing any messages?'

Jenna had been long enough in Scotland to know that messages were what she called shopping. Rosie said that her neighbours who had called him in would get anything she needed, after which the doctor said he'd be back to check up on her in a couple of days.

'Has she no relatives?' wondered Jenna as they returned to the car.

'She's outlived the lot of them,' said Dr William wryly, 'but in a close-knit community like ours the neighbours generally rally round. And now for something completely different.'

Mrs MacKenzie-Smith also had broncho-pneumonia and also lived alone, but in one of the large stone villas Jenna had admired on her way into town yesterday. And instead of shawls and a box bed in the kitchen, she had a pink satin bed-jacket and a mountainous double duvet in a vast centrally heated bedroom.

'Perhaps not so different after all,' mused Jenna as they left the house. 'Ill health is a great leveller.'

'Up to a point, but whereas Rosie has caring neighbours, that old besom upstairs quarrelled with hers years ago. That's why she has to go into a nursing home for a couple of weeks.'

He wasn't so wrong after all about the difference. 'Somewhere there's a moral in all that,' returned Jenna.

'So there is, lassie, and for my money it's do as you would be done by. I think we'll go and see our ex-district nurse next. She usually has the kettle on about this time.'

That morning, they saw nobody who was desperately ill, but all the patients were elderly and some were very frail. As last night with Rob, Jenna was constantly aware of the benefit to patients in having a doctor who knew them so well. 'Like all small isolated communities, Port Lindsay has an ageing population,' Dr William summed up after their last call. 'The boatyard closed down last year and, with the fishing contracting all the time, the young folk are forced to go away if they want work.'

'There must be some who get jobs here, though,' assumed Jenna.

'A few—mostly those with family businesses to go into.'

'Like Rob,' she suggested impulsively.

'Ah!' was Dr William's reply to that, making Jenna wonder if she'd missed the mark, and how. 'I have to ring the nursing home about M'lady MacKenzie-Smith,' he said as they entered the house, 'but you should go and get your lunch, lassie.'

'The doctors never eat much at lunch time,' explained Mrs Cullen when she saw Jenna. 'Just soup and cheese and fruit. I hope that will be sufficient for you too, Doctor,' she added firmly.

Jenna said goodness, yes, after such a large breakfast.

Mrs Cullen sniffed at that. 'At one time, it was fried bacon and egg every morning till we had the collyresterol scare. I don't think there's anything in that myself,' she added, putting a large bowl of vegetable soup in front of Jenna. 'Half the things wrong with folk today are due to not eating enough.'

'In that case, we should all keep healthy in this house,' remarked Jenna. 'This is wonderful soup, Mrs Cullen. Did you make it?'

'Aye. There's no tinned rubbish served in this house,' was the repressive reply.

Having finished her lunch before the other doctors appeared, Jenna decided to go for a short walk as she wasn't needed again until two-thirty. She fetched her warmest coat, tied a woollen scarf over her blonde hair and set off. The houses and buildings of Shore Street were a reflection of the town's fluctuating fortunes, she decided, as she reached the harbour mouth and paused there, looking back. Fishermen's cottages, quayside bars, a ship's chandler's, grim half-ruined warehouses. One or two smart little boutiques, presumably aimed at the summer visitors. A bank, even a building society office, and a surprising number of large houses like the Strachans'. The homes of prosperous merchants perhaps, in the days when Port Lindsay was a thriving port trading with Scandinavia and the Low Countries.

Today, there were many more boats tied up in the harbour. Jenna counted thirty-two before giving up. Were they stormbound? she wondered. It was certainly very windy still. Or was this enforced idleness due to the stringent conservation restrictions on fishing? She must find out all she could about that, when this was a community where nearly everybody depended directly or indirectly on the fishing.

A sudden vicious gust of wind sent Jenna staggering against a great pile of fish boxes. She swore under her breath as a jagged edge tore her tights.

At that, two men deep in conversation near by turned round. 'No serious damage done, I hope,' said one. He was wearing a smart business suit and seemed to be as much out of tune with his surroundings as she was. And very different from his fisherman friend.

'No—nothing serious, thank you,' she returned.

'You're the new doctor,' said the man, giving Jenna

a thorough apppraisal which she found rather flattering.

'News travels fast around here,' she answered with a smile. 'I only arrived yesterday.'

'I know,' he said. 'I saw you from my office window.' He held out a well-manicured hand. 'Nick Lawson of Fergus, Fergus and Lawson, Solicitors.'

Jenna took his hand. 'Jenna Fielding.'

'You're English, Dr Jenna Fielding,' said the man.

'I know, but it's not my fault,' she replied, earning an appreciative chuckle from the other man.

'But it does make me wonder what you're doing here,' persisted the first one.

Jenna wasn't going to explain that to him or anyone else in Port Lindsay! 'Furthering my career in general practice, I hope,' she said. 'Though that could be in doubt if I don't get back to the surgery soon.' She smiled again at both men, turned up her collar against the wind and started back along the quay.

She'd gone barely a dozen yards when Nick Lawson caught up with her. 'You'll have friends in the town,' he assumed.

Jenna said no, not yet, but she lived in hope.

'Then you must let me show you around,' he urged.

Jenna thought that could be rather nice, though not before she'd found out something about him. Having been brought up in a small town in the Yorkshire Dales, she knew the social pitfalls of a small community. 'That's extremely kind of you, but for the moment I have quite a heavy schedule,' she said, smiling just enough to let him see that wasn't meant as a brush-off.

'I believe you,' he returned. 'Rob Strachan is a slave driver. Why else would the last assistant leave before her time was up?'

'The weather perhaps,' suggested Jenna as another spiteful gust of wind sent her reeling again. Nick would have taken her arm then, but she dodged round the far side of a pile of nets. 'Is it always this windy?' she asked.

'Oh, no. On maybe a dozen days every year it's quite calm,' he told her with a wry grin. 'Of course it's less windy inland.'

'Then that's the way I'll be heading on my days off,' said Jenna as they arrived back at Harbour House. 'Thanks for your company,' she said lightly. 'It's been nice talking to you.'

He eyed her assessingly. 'See you around,' he said at last.

Jenna paused on the top step, key in hand. 'In a small place like this, I should think that's more than likely,' she answered, smiling. He might ring her and he might not. Jenna rather hoped he would. What better way of taking her mind off Jake than going out with another man?

'Dr Rob has been asking for you,' called Mrs Cullen as Jenna crossed the hall.

Jenna looked at her watch. Blast! Half-two already. 'Thank you, Mrs Cullen. I'll go through as soon as I've put my coat away.'

'You can leave it on the hall stand.'

'I also wish to go to the bathroom,' returned Jenna, determined not to go running as Mrs Cullen thought she ought.

'Ah, hum, yes,' said Mrs Cullen, going back to her kitchen and shutting the door with a bang. She didn't approve of young women who said things right out like that—even if they were doctors.

Rob already had a patient in the consulting-room when Jenna joined him. 'I had hoped for a brief discussion first,' he said. 'But I suppose you can always read my preliminary notes.'

'I'll do that,' agreed Jenna calmly. They weren't very enlightening; just the patient's name, age, marital status and mention of a three-month history of increasing lassitude and some weight loss. That could portend all manner of things—including a failed relationship, as she knew full well. She settled in a corner, prepared to watch and listen.

Rob was very thorough in his examination. Heart, lungs, abdomen—merely observing didn't tell her much, although she could admire his technique. His questions were more helpful. He suspects the kidneys, decided Jenna, confirmed in that suspicion when he mentioned samples of blood and urine for analysis.

'Would it help if I dealt with those, Dr Strachan?' she asked in an effort to be useful.

He started at the sound of her voice, as though he'd forgotten she was there. Very flattering! 'Thank you, Dr Fielding, but the laboratory van has already called for today's samples for in-depth analysis, so I'll be asking her to come back tomorrow morning early. As for the urine, I took the precaution of asking her to bring a sample with her when I gave her this appointment.'

'So what is wrong with me then, Doctor?' asked the patient, seizing her chance.

'The most likely thing is a chronic infection, Mrs Patterson,' he told her blandly, 'so we'll start you on a course of antibiotics and see how you are in a fortnight.'

'An infection? Like the flu, do you mean?'

'In as much as flu is an infection,' he returned obliquely.

'Why do you need a blood sample, then, if you know

what's the matter with me?' she persisted. 'I have the weans to take to school in the morn. . .'

'It'll not be much out of your way,' urged Rob, 'and I'll only keep you a moment. It'll help to make sure we've chosen the right medicine.' He handed her a prescription. 'Start that today now—and make an appointment on your way out for morning surgery today fortnight.'

'Right, Doctor! Diagnosis please,' he said to Jenna as the patient's footsteps echoed down the passage.

'Bearing in mind that I haven't examined her,' Jenna began carefully, 'I would think that chronic pyelonephritis is the most likely. That so-called cystitis she mentioned under your prompting could have been an acute attack—which of course went untreated. So—'

'Good thinking. So what would you have done for her?'

'Put her on ampicillin as you did.'

'Anything else?'

'I think I'd get her a hospital appointment to exclude any other renal pathology.'

'You *think*?'

Jenna was getting irritated. Did he have to treat her like some green student? 'I was *trying* to be diplomatic, Doctor. If she were my patient, I shouldn't hesitate to refer her.'

'I'm glad to hear it—and of course I'll be doing that. Unfortunately, there's usually a delay of several weeks, so I'm saving that news for nearer the time. Mention hospital to a worrier like Nan Patterson, and she'll worry herself silly in the interim.'

'Another example of the benefit of knowing one's patients well,' said Jenna quietly.

He shrugged. 'If you like.' He bent down and put the patient's urine sample out of sight. 'Let's hope that doesn't tell us anything unpleasant when we examine it later. And now for something completely different.' He looked sharply at Jenna when she smothered a chuckle.

'Your father said that very thing to me on his rounds this morning.'

'Must be something in the genes, then,' he said, ringing the bell for Meg to send in the next patient.

A neurological problem this time; another meticulous and thorough examination of his and one which wouldn't have disgraced a consultant neurologist. Jenna found herself wondering how long he had been a GP—and what he'd been doing before that. He prescribed the patient some muscle relaxants and told her he was making an appointment for her to see a nerve specialist.

When she had gone, Jenna asked why the hospital referral when the diagnosis of multiple sclerosis was all too clear.

'Because she needs physiotherapy and can only get it on a consultant's say-so.'

Jenna was amazed. 'What a waste of time,' she breathed. 'In Edinburgh, most hospital physio departments accept direct GP referrals.'

His expression was enough to make her sorry she'd opened her mouth, even before she'd finished. 'Is that a fact?' he asked woodenly. 'Well, I'm sorry to tell you that doesn't happen here.' He didn't elaborate and Jenna didn't ask him to. She stuffed her hands in the pockets of her white coat and fixed her eyes on the blind-cord behind his head. Perhaps that had been an unwise observation on her part, but how was she to know how things were done here if nobody told her and she didn't ask? One thing was sure. It was to Dr

William she'd be going for information in future—not to his arrogant, antagonistic son!

'I think you'll find our last patient very interesting,' said Rob, breaking in on her thoughts. 'He's a boy of nine, and with the family being new to the town I know nothing about him.'

So we'll be level-pegging on this one, thought Jenna as Meg ushered in mother and child.

It was indeed an interesting case. The boy had severe behavioural problems as well as bizarre ritualistic movements.

'Any ideas?' asked Rob when the child and his mother had gone.

Jenna had listened carefully to all the questions and answers and her suspicions couldn't possibly fit in with what she'd heard, so she said briefly, 'No, none.'

'What—none at all?' he persisted in a very superior way.

'None that fits in with the information—as far as it went.'

'Can we possibly be thinking along the same lines?' he wondered.

If they were, it was a first. . . 'Possibly,' said Jenna, determined not to stick her neck out again. She fixed her eyes anew on that blind-cord.

'You're not very forthcoming this time, Doctor,' said her tormentor.

She took a deep breath and looked straight at him, her green eyes cool. 'Very well, then, I think that child is suffering from a very rare syndrome—one with an hereditary basis. Genetic,' she emphasised. 'But your exhaustive questioning failed to uncover any other cases on either side of the family. So the inescapable conclusion is that the boy's parents are not his biological parents.'

'I'm very impressed, Dr Fielding,' he said. 'You could have been forgiven for not picking that up.'

'Perhaps—I prefer to think not.' Jenna was virtually seething now, but was determined to keep her temper. 'The important thing is that the diagnosis is made and now that child will be getting the expert treatment he needs.' Another deep breath. 'Are there any more cases for this session, Doctor? Because if not, I'd rather like to get to the Post Office before closing time.'

'I'm afraid you're out of luck,' he said—and, sounding quite smug, she thought, 'Thursday is early-closing day in Port Lindsay.'

'Really?' Jenna was sure she had him this time. 'Then how, one wonders, can our kidney patient start her antibiotics today, as you told her to?'

The smug look actually increased. 'Because the town has two chemist shops and the one that shuts on Wednesday will be open today.'

Jenna caught her bottom lip between even pearly teeth. 'How very convenient,' she admitted grudgingly.

'As you say—but don't look so glum, Doctor. Nobody expects you to know everything about the town from the word go.'

'I should hope not,' Jenna answered tightly. 'And, that being so, perhaps a little less one-upmanship every time I show my ignorance would be—charitable.'

He drew in his breath with an audible hiss, but Jenna didn't wait for the crushing reply he'd be sure to make. Mrs Cullen met her in the hall with the news that tea was ready, but Jenna insisted she wasn't hungry and hurried up to her room to think.

She'd been here less that twenty-four hours, though in some ways it felt more like a month. No wonder there'd been no other takers for this posting. She'd assumed that was down to the remoteness of the place.

Now she decided it was all to do with Dr Strachan junior. He was a good and dedicated doctor, but what an impossible man! So determined always to have the last word. In order to demonstrate his authority—or because he feared to lose it?

No, it couldn't be that; the man was so commanding. And, to be fair, he seemed quite reasonable with everybody else. There had to be something about her that he found irritating. All right, so she hadn't exactly taken to him. Such instant mutual antipathy must be close to a record. A great pity, but nobody could say she hadn't shown restraint. But could she keep it up if he went on treating her like a newly qualified houseman?

She was roused from her absorption by a sharp rat-tat on her door. She went to open it, chin up and eyes glinting, but it was only Mrs Cullen hovering on the landing with a tray.

'Dr William's orders,' she said. 'He says you're needing to put your feet up for a bit and it's a long time till supper. He's taking evening surgery, and you're welcome to join him if you want.'

'Please say I'll certainly do that, Mrs Cullen. And thank you for my tea.'

'Dr William insisted,' said the housekeeper tonelessly.

Jenna would have known it wasn't her idea without the explanation and she appreciated the old doctor's thoughtfulness. He had to be aware that his son disliked the new assistant, and was probably trying to keep contact between them to a minimum. Well, keeping to her room would be no hardship when somebody had made it so comfortable.

* * *

Jenna was prompt getting to surgery, but Dr William was already with his first patient. 'Come in, Dr Fielding, and meet one of our best customers,' he greeted her. Judging by the thickness of the folder open on the desk, he wasn't joking.

'You name it, I've had it, Dr Fielding,' confirmed the patient complacently.

Jenna almost sympathised, before realising there was no need; Mrs Taggart so obviously enjoyed the distinction. Today she had a ringing in her ears and darting pains in her legs to report and wanted to know if there was any connection. Dr William said he'd be surprised if there was, told her she was a walking miracle, all things considered, and sent her away happy.

'Every week as regular as clockwork,' he said when she'd gone. 'Well, we all need our props in life, and a visit to the doctor for a compliment and a bit of reassurance is less harmful than cigarettes or too many trips to the bottle.'

It was a novel perception of a GP's role but there was a lot of truth in it, as Jenna told him. 'Medicine is as much about kindness and understanding as it is about diagnosis and treatment,' she added.

Dr William replied that she was shaping up to be a doctor he could thoroughly approve of and they waited for their next patient in much greater harmony than had been present in that room earlier in the day.

Except for a prickly problem like lonely Wilma Smith, the surgery was a re-run of the one the previous night. 'Not much there to stretch a bright girl like you, Jenna,' apologised Dr William when the consulting-room door closed behind the last customer.

'But isn't that what general practice is all about?' she asked. 'We lose all our absorbing cases to the hospital.'

Dr William agreed up to a point. 'But a general

practitioner needs to be a good diagnostician if he's to know when to call on the hospital facilities.' He paused. 'Rob was telling me at teatime about your brilliant diagnosis of that child.'

Jenna was thrilled to hear that, but she played it down. 'Actually, I saw a similar child during my recent spell on paediatrics, and it's the sort of case which sticks in one's mind. Anyway, he'd already made the diagnosis himself.

'He also told me how you picked up that pyelonephritis.'

'That was obvious too,' she claimed.

'I wonder?' mused the old man. 'You really mustn't put yourself down, Jenna. Nobody will praise you for it.'

Was he telling her to stand up to Rob? 'I can stick up for myself when I need to,' she assured him. Professionally anyway, she reflected with a tiny pang as she remembered how desperately weak she'd been about standing up to Jake over the years. . .

But he was telling her how glad he was to hear that. 'And now let's go and see what Mrs Cullen has got for our supper. It's just the two of us tonight. She likes her meal earlier, and as this is Rob's half-day he's dining with friends.' Some half-day, when he spent the afternoon working. . . 'And yours will be Wednesday, if that suits you,' added Dr William.

'Anything that suits you will suit me, Doctor,' Jenna assured him. 'And after supper—if you can be bothered—I'd really like you to tell me something about the town and its people. Just so that I don't tread on too many toes. I'd hate to do that.'

'I can't imagine you being insensitive, Jenna,' he said, 'but I'll certainly list any obvious pitfalls that occur to me, if you think that would be helpful.'

So later, over coffee in the sitting-room, Jenna got her briefing. The Carswells of Fisher's Wynd were a very chesty family and the Braids much given to strokes. Tam Ritchie was a card and endlessly ingenious when he wanted a sick note, which was a least once a month when Forfar were playing at home. Definitely one to watch out for. Mostly, though, it was the opposite problem and the good folk of Port Lindsay had to be wrested from their work when unfit for it.

'You have a great affection for these people,' realised Jenna after an hour or more of fascinating anecdotes.

'They're my ain folk,' said Dr William simply. 'My grandfather was a fisherman and so was my father, until he realised he could make more money building boats for other men to take to sea.'

There was one man she'd met who hadn't yet been mentioned and when she got the chance, Jenna said casually, 'I went for a walk after lunch and got into conversation with a man who told me he was a solicitor. Lawson, I think he said his name was. . .'

'That would be young Nick,' Dr William said readily. 'Strictly speaking, he's not a Port Lindsayite at all, having been brought up in Aberdeen. The senior partner, old Jack Fergus, is his grandfather and he leaves most of the work to the boy. Nick is very bright.'

Nothing there to his detriment—unless it was his 'foreign' upbringing! Well, she was a foreigner too, so they were alike in that respect. Would Rob Strachan be annoyed if she made a friend of Nick Lawson? Jenna rather hoped he would!

CHAPTER THREE

'AT LEAST you got your supper in peace, Jenna,' said Dr William when the phone rang just as they were having coffee. This was Jenna's third Friday in Port Lindsay and her first weekend on call. There had been a bit of an argument about that. Rob had said she needed more time to get to know the area, while she suspected it was more a matter of trust—or lack of it—on his part. But, knowing how much Jenna resented Rob's nannying, William had put his foot down.

'Yes. What nice considerate patients we have,' she laughed as she picked up the phone. 'Dr Fielding here. Can I help you?' she asked briskly, pen and paper at the ready.

'Yes please, Doctor,' said Nick. 'I haven't seen you for all of three days, so how about dinner tomorrow?'

Had she been alone, she'd have thanked him before saying, 'Sorry, but I'm on duty this weekend.'

'And don't you eat when you're on duty?' he asked whimsically.

'Yes, of course, but——'

'Let me have that,' said Rob, getting up and holding out his hand for the phone.

Jenna stared at him. 'No. Why should I?'

He frowned down on her. 'Because the quickest way to deal with a reluctant patient is for me to explain the new system.'

He thought that Nick was a patient expressing a preference for a Strachan! 'This is a personal call—for me,' she stated firmly.

He looked embarrassed, something she'd never expected to see.

'Sorry,' he apologised gruffly. 'I thought——'

'I know,' said Jenna, turning her back on him. 'Sorry about that,' she said into the phone. 'A slight misunderstanding at this end.'

'And I bet I know who caused it,' he said. 'Now listen, if you'd really rather not, then please say so, but you have to eat somewhere, work or no work, so what about it? There's a very decent little restaurant right here on the waterfront. Or I could do you an omelette at my place. . .'

'I rather like the sound of the first alternative,' she said, because there wasn't really any reason why she shouldn't dine out as long as she could be reached by phone.

'Great!' he responded, loud enough to be heard by the others. 'I'll call for you at half-seven.'

'No, don't do that,' she interposed quickly. 'I might be out on a call. Just tell me where, and I'll meet you—work permitting. If not, I'll leave a message.'

'You've done this before,' he laughed.

'Once or twice,' she confirmed. 'It rather goes with the job.' He named the restaurant, not more than a hundred yards away, told her he was longing to see her, and rang off.

Rob had recovered from his slight embarrassment. 'Let's hope no patient was trying to get through during all that,' he remarked stolidly.

Jenna resumed her seat at the table and eyed him calmly. 'If so I'm sure they'll have the sense to ring again. Just as the man with the sprained ankle did after Mrs Cullen was on the phone for so long before supper.' And you didn't make a song and dance about *that*, she added silently.

'Mrs Cullen was using the private line,' Rob revealed smugly, leaving Jenna to smart at being outwitted yet again.

She wasted no more words on Rob, but asked William if she had his permission to give her friends the ex-directory number for future use. He said good heavens yes and he hadn't realised she didn't know it already. Jenna then thanked him fulsomely for Rob's benefit and hoped the incident was closed.

Not so. After William went early to bed, pleading fatigue, Rob laid aside the crossword puzzle he'd been frowning over since supper and said carefully, 'I understood you to say you didn't know anybody in Port Lindsay.'

'I didn't—when I arrived.'

'You've not been here three weeks yet. You make friends very quickly.'

'Sometimes—yes. There are people one takes to right away and others—one just doesn't. Anyway, what makes you think that was a local call earlier?'

He didn't answer, but got up to put another log on the fire before saying hesitantly, 'I don't quite know how to say this, but——'

'Whenever I hear that, I know that something better left unsaid is coming,' warned Jenna.

He acknowledged the truth of that with a thin smile. 'All the same. . .'

Jenna folded her arms across her chest and eyed him steadily. He was definitely going to say something unpleasant, so he'd not be getting any help from her.

'It *was* Nick Lawson who rang you, was it not?'

'I knew you'd recognised his voice.'

'He hasn't taken long to scrape up an acquaintance. But then he never does.'

'That must be because he has such an outgoing personality.'

She was being deliberately provocative and why not? He was behaving like an old-fashioned schoolmarm!

Rob uttered a derisive snort. 'That's one way of describing him!'

'Yes—my way,' she retorted. 'But obviously you see him differently. If you know something to his discredit—something that makes it inadvisable for me to go on seeing him—then be good enough to tell me without any more bush-beating.'

'He's very—impressionable.'

'Most men are, in my experience.' And Jake most of all. . .

He eyed her blonde prettiness morosely. 'I can believe that. Look. I'm not trying to interfere——'

'Huh!' snorted Jenna in her turn.

He stuck his thumbs in the waistband of his jeans and glared down at her. 'It's obviously no good trying to talk to you while you're in this mood,' he said heavily, 'but when he drops you to go chasing after the next new face in town, don't say I didn't warn you!'

'I won't,' agreed Jenna. 'How could I? You have!' She got to her feet, returning glare for glare. 'I am going to my room!' she snapped, heading for the door.

'Then don't forget to switch the phone through,' he shouted after her; a reminder all the more annoying because she hadn't thought of it herself.

On present showing, it would probably have been safe to have a bath, but more that five years in hospital had conditioned Jenna to rapid showering only when on call. Besides, she had a shower in her room, whereas going for a bath meant the risk of Rob rattling the door-handle and going off in a huff. A spot of telephone eavesdropping of her own had revealed that he too had a date that night.

So far, this had been a very easy weekend. Only seven patients for morning surgery and just five visits in the afternoon. Now she was really looking forward to her evening and the only puzzle was what to wear. This Lobster Pot place wouldn't be as grand as that fancy hotel Nick had taken her to last Saturday, so her printed wool skirt with the pure silk dark emerald shirt should fit the bill. Especially with some beads and jangly earrings. Jenna then shrugged on her warmest coat, tied a scarf over her head—that ruddy wind hadn't abated one jot these past three days—and, waiting only to pop a recorded message in the answering machine, she set off for the restaurant. Daft to take the car, but if there should be a call it would save coming back for it.

Nick was already there and had a gin and tonic waiting for her. 'It's a very weak one,' he assured her, smiling into her eyes. 'I know the score.'

She was reminded that her predecessor had been a woman. Had he given her the treatment too, then? Damn you, Rob Strachan, for trying to sour this for me. Well, I'm not going to let you! 'I'm so glad,' she said, smiling back.

'You like gin and tonic,' he assumed.

'Love it—and I also like a man who knows the score. It saves boring explanations.'

'I couldn't live the way you doctors do,' said Nick.

'And I'd probably go mad trying to fathom all that legal jargon,' returned Jenna, looking round appreciatively. 'I like this place, Nick. I'd never expected anything quite so—so. . .' She didn't want to sound patronising.

'Stylish?' he finished for her. 'It's only been open a few months and it's very popular.'

'I can see that,' she agreed as they followed a waitress to their table. It was already more that half full, and an elaborately decorated table in an alcove suggested it was the in-place for celebrations.

Nick was friendly, easy to talk to and not nearly as pushy as Jenna had wondered if he might be, that first day. They were absorbed in an exchange of life stories when a party of four came to claim the fancy table in the alcove; two dark, vivacious women who were obviously sisters, a burly thick-set man who looked like a farmer—and Rob.

It didn't take long to decide that the more elegantly dressed woman was married to the farmer. Or that her sister had designs on Rob. I'd be ashamed if I couldn't keep my hands to myself better than that, Jenna thought scornfully, the fourth time the girl ran her hand down his arm. Though, to be fair, he wasn't exactly discouraging her. She'd never seen him smiling like that. It made him quite handsome—no, positively attractive!

'I know this chocolate roulade is good,' Nick said plaintively, 'but you haven't said a single word since they brought it!' He'd also noticed her glancing past his shoulder and turned round to see why. He whistled. 'No wonder! Your boss's presence must be very inhibiting.'

'Nonense! Anyway, he isn't my boss—his father is. It's the women who interest me. They're so striking. Do you know who they are?'

'They're the MacArthur sisters. Daddy is a rich farmer and Shelagh did the right thing by marrying the owner of the rolling acres next door. Susan, on the other hand, would seem to have less rustic inclinations. At a guess, I'd say they're all here celebrating Shelagh and Dougal's fifth wedding anniversary. Even something else,' he added when Susan caressed Rob's sleeve yet again.

'It must be fascinating to be a lawyer and know everybody's business,' trilled Jenna satirically.

'That's a laugh! Who better placed than a doctor to collect murky secrets?'

'You're right,' she said. 'What wonderful chances for blackmail in both our professions.'

'I hope you're not suggesting——' he was saying when he was interrupted by the waitress who came to say she was awful sorry, but Dr Fielding was wanted on the phone.

'An emergency, I guess,' Jenna said ruefully to Nick as she followed the girl to a small cubicle beside the bar. Curious eyes from all sides followed her progress.

Jenna picked up the phone. 'Dr Fielding here. . .'

'It's Mother, Doctor,' said an agitated female voice. 'She tripped over the dog and went her length and now she can't get up.'

'Name and address, please,' said Jenna. Anxious callers had been known to ring off before you could get that vital information.

'Goodall. Thirty-five Seaview Terrace. The council houses. You go up——'

'Yes, thanks—I know where that is. Is your mother elderly?'

'Aye, seventy-nine past. And she's awful shocked, Doctor.'

A fractured neck of femur, Jenna feared. 'That's only to be expected,' she said bracingly. 'Keep her warm, but don't try to move her. I'll be there directly.'

Jenna found her coat and went back to Nick. 'Sounds

quite serious, I'm afraid, so there's no knowing how long I'll be. And we were having such a lovely time—I'm sorry. . .' But her thoughts were way ahead, with her patient.

He was very good about it. 'You did warn me. Do you think you'll be back?'

'Best not to expect me.'

'I've nothing else to do,' he said, but she was already on her way. She'd quite forgotten Rob and his friends, but his eyes followed her to the door, speculating.

She found the house without any trouble, having visited the one opposite with William. It only took a minute to confirm Jenna's gloomy suspicions of a fracture inside the hip joint, a serious injury for somebody of that age. She replaced the blanket round the patient, explaining gently that when you hurt your hip it was best to get it X-rayed. Then she got to her feet to say to the patient's daughter in a low voice, 'I'm afraid she's broken her hip and that means hospital and an operation. Do you have a phone, or—?'

'Over here, Doctor.'

Having ordered the ambulance, Jenna returned to her patient, who was beginning to fret. 'I'm going to give her something to settle her and make her comfy for the trip.' Perhaps ten minutes in the city but probably five times that long here. . . 'When did she last eat?'

'We all had fish and chips about six, Doctor.'

So with luck she'd not be sick on the way. 'I've done all I can,' said Jenna, 'and you'll be wanting to pack a case for her. Besides, there may be other calls coming in, and this time I'm not at the number on the answering machine.'

'I'd not like your job, Doctor. All this weekend work.'

'And I wouldn't like any other,' smiled Jenna. 'Ambulance control promised to be here for your mother in twenty minutes, but if they don't show up in the next half-hour, ring Harbour House and I'll chase them up.'

'We'll do that, Doctor—and thanks ever so much for coming.'

'All part of the service,' said Jenna. Her instinct about another call had been right. Switching on the answering machine she heard a message from Rosie's neighbour saying that she'd fallen out of bed and was groaning something shocking.

Out to the car again and off to the other side of the harbour. Rosie was bruised and angry, but, her being much better padded than thin little Mrs Goodall, no serious damage was done. Just as well. 'I'm no' going to hospital,' she kept repeating.

'No, no—of course not. There's no need,' Jenna repeated just as often.

'When folk my age go in there, they dinnae come oot.'

'Of course they do, Rosie, or the place would have stopped admitting years ago.'

'And who said you could call me Rosie? I'm Mrs Meldrum to you, ye cheeky besom.'

'So sorry, Mrs Meldrum—I'm forgetting my manners. Now what would you say to a nice cup of tea?'

'I'd rather have a dram. In yon cupboard there—next the stove.'

'All right,' agreed Jenna. A dram would do as well as a sedative and be a sight more palatable. 'Only a wee one, though.'

'Och away! I could drink a wee lassie like you under the table any time.'

Jenna didn't doubt that—or that Rosie had recovered in record time from the shock of her fall.

But going home again, she began to worry. Just supposing Rosie had cracked a bone after all? Rob would never let her forget it. But she hasn't—I know she hasn't. I *must* trust my own judgement. I'll visit her again tomorrow morning though—just to make absolutely sure. . .

There were no more messages on the answering machine, so Jenna switched the phone through to her room and went to bed. She was never quite relaxed when on call though, and it was well after two before she dozed off. She still hadn't heard Rob come in.

Despite his late night, Rob got to the breakfast table before Jenna. He didn't look particularly jaded either, but then doctors everywhere got by on less than the average amount of sleep.

Jenna had decided not to mention seeing him at the Lobster Pot, but he wasn't so sensitive. 'Your dinner date was interrupted last night,' he remarked as soon as they'd exchanged good mornings.

Jenna shrugged. 'Not really—I only missed the coffee. How is your father today?'

'Still asleep, according to Jeannie.'

'Sleep is a great healer,' Jenna said fatuously, appalling herself.

'I'm disappointed,' Rob said emphatically.

'I beg your pardon?'

'I'd never thought to hear such a platitude from one with your way with words.'

'Forgive me. I'm never at my best first thing in the morning.'

'So you're more of an evening sparkler, are you?'

'I can do my share of sparkling at any time—given the right company,' she answered pointedly.

'Which you certainly had last night, judging by the way you were behaving.'

'I wouldn't have thought you'd have any attention to spare,' murmured Jenna, buttering some toast.

'Meaning?'

'When I'm out with friends, I don't waste time watching the other diners.'

'Oh, come! The odd glance or two. . .'

Jenna flushed faintly. He'd seen her glancing at those two women, hadn't he, the brute? 'I suppose it does rather depend on whom one is with,' she said, not entirely sure what she meant by that.

As always, Rob put the least favourable construction on her remark. 'So he was boring you, then, was he?' he asked with a provocative smirk.

'I've seldom been less bored in my life,' Jenna retorted roundly. 'Nick Lawson is excellent company. Meeting him was a tremendous stroke of luck.' Careful, Jenna. That was rather over the top.

'If you say so.' Rob poured himself more coffee, remembering to ask if she wanted any.

'No, thank you. I'm going to work now.'

'Where? No calls have come in yet this morning.'

'I'm going to visit a couple of patients I saw yesterday.'

'Why?' he pounced. 'Were you in doubt about diagnosis? If so, I'll—'

Jenna had to clench her fists very hard to curb the impulse to hit him hard. 'Of course I'm in doubt,' she said through stiff lips. 'I've only been qualified five and a half years, held SHO and junior registrar posts right across the board *and* managed to pass my MRCP exam. So how can I claim to be competent enough to treat a common cold?' she wound up in a voice trembling with indignation.

She expected him to say she was hysterical, before prescribing valium and a nice lie down, but instead he asked incredulously, 'You've got your MRCP?'

'But only because I bribed the examiners. How else?' she demanded crossly, pushing roughly past him in her haste to get out of the room.

She didn't calm down until she'd fetched her coat, collected her bag and switched on the answering machine—and thank heaven she'd remembered to do that! Then she ran to her car and went to visit Rosie.

She found her up, dressed and feeding her cats. There was a blazing fire in the kitchen and a scuttle full of coal by the stove. The outside stair was slippery with rain as well as very worn, and Jenna asked anxiously who had brought in the coal.

'Jeemsie from next door. He always fills ma scuttle of a morn.'

'I'm very glad to hear that—that stair of yours is dangerous. How's your leg this morning, Mrs Meldrum?'

Rosie curled her lip. 'I thocht it was ma chest that was supposed to be bad. Dr William says——'

'I came to see you last night because you'd hurt your leg. Don't you remember?'

'Och, that—a lot o' nonsense for a wee bittie bruising!' She actually did a few clumsy dance steps. 'See?'

'And you've no pain at all?'

'Ye can be sure I'd tell ye if I had.'

'I just happened to be passing, so I thought I'd make quite sure,' Jenna explained.

'Passing, ye say,' returned Rosie satirically. 'Where to?'

And a very good question too, when her cottage was almost the last one before the harbour entrance.

'Sorry—that's a professional secret,' said Jenna,

made quite happy again by Rosie's obvious escape from serious injury.

Now for a check on yesterday afternoon's suspected heart attack. Almost certainly nothing more than severe indigestion, but best to be sure. . . What do I mean, Jenna asked herself indignantly. I *am* sure! Damn you, Rob Strachan—you'd have the Pope himself doubting his judgement!

Jenna was just in time to catch her heart dyspepsia patient sitting down to a greasy breakfast of bacon and eggs. 'What about that diet sheet I gave you yesterday, Mr Black?' she asked reproachfully.

'I'll maybe take a look at it tomorrow, m'lass.'

Her green eyes flashed fire. Oh, he would, would he? 'I am not your lass, Mr Black, I'm your doctor!'

'Och, awa' back to yer knittin', lassie,' he said then. 'Dr Rob's ma doctor.'

The green eyes flashed some more. 'Then I suggest you make an early appointment with him for a complete check-up. You are grossly overweight and seriously under-exercised, so the next time you think you're having a heart attack, you may very well be right!' And with that, Jenna bounced furiously out of the room.

Out in the cold wind, she cooled down a bit. He deserved to be told that, but not in quite such vicious terms. He had his precious Dr Rob to blame for that. If he hadn't watched her and harried her and pounced on every tiny hesitancy or minor difference of approach, the way he had ever since she arrived, then she'd never have been reduced to doubting herself so much that she double-checked every diagnosis she made.

All the same, the way that man had spoken to her was outrageous. Away back to your knitting indeed! Jenna was learning fast that the way folk felt free to speak to you in their homes was vastly different from their attitude in hospital, where doctors were on their own ground. Or was it more than that? Had Dr Rob's tacit disapproval of women doctors rubbed off on the patients? If so, life here was going to be even more difficult that she'd thought.

When Jenna got back to Harbour House, there was nobody in and no calls on the answering machine. She wondered what Nick was doing. On impulse, she rang his number but only got a recorded message. She thanked him for last night, switched the phone over and went to her room. There, she crossed to the front windows and looked out on the boats in the harbour. The only sign of activity was on the lifeboat slip. The sea beyond the harbour wall looked angry and menacing. Were they planning an exercise, or was that launch for real?

Jenna had never before been so conscious of the sea; had never lived near it, or among people whose living it was. She was very conscious of being an outsider. Most people so far had been polite, one or two—like Nick—even welcoming, but this was going to be a difficult year. If she survived that long. She cursed again the impulse that had driven her to put the greatest possible distance between herself and Jake.

A call to a farm some way inland spared Jenna the embarrassment of sharing Sunday lunch with Rob so soon after her outburst at breakfast. And then worrying about what she would find when she got there stopped her thinking about all the trouble she was in.

According to the farmer, his daughter—a keen show-jumper—had been schooling a new horse and taken a bit of a tumble. Nobody had seen her fall and the girl herself had been too dazed to remember exactly what happened. The first the family knew of it was when the horse returned riderless to its box.

'And when was this?' asked Jenna keenly.

'About half-nine—maybe ten,' the girl returned casually. They were all keen riders in that house and inclined to shrug off falls as par for the course.

'But it's well after one now,' realised Jenna with a frown.

'Yes—and I'm fine now. Dad only phoned because Mum thought he should.'

Jenna realised she'd only been called in to say that all was well but she couldn't do that. Apart from the girl's temporary amnesia, there were no specific signs of injury, but Jenna had a feeling; the sort of sixth sense that every doctor got once in a while. 'I want Belinda to go to hospital for X-rays and observation,' she said firmly.

'Oh, come now, Doctor. Look at her,' urged the father. 'Anybody can see she's fine now.'

Belinda seconded that.

'Where's the phone?' Jenna asked doggedly. 'I'm going to call an ambulance.'

'Och, there's no need for that. One of her brothers will take her—if you insist.'

If you don't conveniently forget all about it when I've gone! 'No,' said Jenna firmly. 'It's more than thirty miles to the hospital from here and Belinda may very well be sick on the way. People often are after a bang of the head.'

Jenna was allowed to phone, but grudgingly, and then the father said, 'You'll be wanting to get away now, Doctor. Sorry to call you out for nothing on a Sunday, but you know how it is. Her mother. . .'

He's the sort of man who'll always blame his wife, thought Jenna. What with one thing and another, she was feeling decidedly anti-male today. 'Not for nothing, I assure you,' she insisted quietly. 'And I intend to wait until the ambulance comes.'

'What about your other patients?' persisted the man.

'After calling the ambulance, I took the liberty of phoning Harbour House. They know where to reach me if I'm needed.'

He could hardly turn her out, but he didn't have to stay and talk to the confounded woman, so he went off, muttering, to his den.

Jenna put in the time writing a note for the ambulance crew to give to the duty casualty officer, as Belinda couldn't give any account of her fall. The ambulance arrived some twenty minutes later and Jenna followed after it down the bumpy track, getting back to the house just before three.

'Another call came in for you about ten minutes back,' was Mrs Cullen's greeting. 'I made a note of the name and address.'

'Thank you,' returned Jenna, swallowing a sigh. By now she was very hungry. She took the note and went through to the surgery to get the patient's notes out. He proved to be that Tam Ritchie, the ingenious fabricator of reasons for sick notes, of whom Dr William had warned her. But as soon as she saw his hand, Jenna knew there was no need for invention today. 'How did this happen, Mr Ritchie?' she asked as she opened her bag for dressings and antiseptic.

'I was holding a nail for ma brother and he misfired wi' the hammer,' he said matter-of-factly, histrionics unnecessary.

'He must pack a fair old punch then,' she said grimly. 'This is definitely a hospital job.'

He waited until Jenna had swabbed the wound clean and dressed it before saying, 'You've made a gey neat job of it, Doctor, so mebbe we could forget the hospital.'

But Jenna insisted and the hammer-wielding brother agreed to drive the casualty.

Jenna asked how those patients without cars managed and was told that they just had to take the bus. 'And that can take two hours or more,' added Tam. 'Yon townies dinnae ken they're born, Doctor.'

'I'm beginning to think that myself,' agreed Jenna, as she repacked her bag.

Back at Harbour House, she found a note from Mrs Cullen on the kitchen table. 'Your lunch is in the Aga and it's ruined,' it said. By then Jenna was hungry enough to eat anything, so she put the plates on a tray, fetched a book on head injuries from the surgery and went upstairs to her room. She was almost sure that everybody was out, but she still didn't feel ready for her next encounter with Rob.

She read as she ate and was confirmed in her decision to send Belinda to hospital. All the same, she wished she hadn't put that list of possible injuries in her note for the staff. In imagination she heard some overworked neurosurgeon muttering, 'Officious ruddy GP,' as he read it. Hadn't she heard similar remarks during her stint on Casualty? It would have been enough just to refer the girl. Still, the fact that she'd done the right thing was what really mattered.

No more calls came in. Jenna read the whole chapter on head injuries and then wrote three letters. After that she had nothing to do but brood.

Would Rob Strachan ever trust her? And if he didn't, would her confidence survive a year in this place? And why the hell does having his good opinion *matter* so much? she was asking herself when she heard the phone ringing downstairs. She leapt to her feet on the instant, realising that she'd forgotten to switch it through to her room. She had to get to it before Rob did, or she'd never hear the last of it.

Too late. It stopped as she stepped down into the hall. She prayed for it to be the private phone but no. Rob's voice was coming from the kitchen and very clearly she heard him say, 'If you'll hold the line, I'll try to find her for you.'

'I'm very sorry,' she muttered defensively when they met in the doorway.

He raised a quizzical eyebrown and said mildly, 'Mr Fraser, the senior consultant neurosurgeon at the district hospital, would like to speak to you.'

Now what? she wondered in a panic as she picked up the phone and quavered, 'G-good evening. Dr Fielding speaking.'

'Michael Fraser here.' What a nice voice, she thought. 'You were spot-on in your diagnosis of that girl. She came over drowsy on the way and was almost unconscious when I saw her. I've just removed a subdural haematoma from the base of the skull and I want to congratulate you.'

Jenna was conscious of the sudden lifting of the clouds. 'Thank you very much—I appreciate this. She seemed all right when I saw her—there were none of the usual signs—but I had this feeling. . .'

'One does,' he said, 'and thank God for it. Well, I mustn't keep you; Rob tells me it's your weekend on. But I couldn't let this pass without a word of praise. Well done, Doctor. Let me know if those Strachans don't treat you right. I'm looking for a good registrar.'

A joke surely, but a compliment too and a very nice one. Jenna thanked him again and said she'd remember that if she found that general practice wasn't for her.

He made another nice remark; something about her

being an asset to any branch of medicine she chose before hanging up and leaving Jenna dazed but jubliant. There was only one cloud in her sky. She could never tell Rob Strachan how complimentary Mr Fraser had been because he'd never believe her. Still, the fact that the man had rung at all must have told him something. Unless he'd assumed she was getting a rocket. Jenna feared that was all too likely.

Rob was standing in the doorway of the sitting-room when she crossed the hall. She had her foot on the first step of the stairs by the time he'd cleared his throat to ask her in the politest way possible if she'd care for a sherry before supper.

Jenna turned round to stare at him. 'No—thank you, Doctor. I'm on duty.'

'I know that,' he returned, sounding more like his usual prickly self. 'But a very small one couldn't do any harm.'

She eyed him sideways, green eyes narrowed, because he had to be up to something. 'I expect you're right,' she said at last. 'All the same, I don't think I will—if you don't mind.'

He shrugged. 'Suit yourself.'

Jenna took two more steps up and then he said jocularly, 'That was quite some coup you pulled off.'

Jenna stopped dead. So Mr Fraser *had* told him why he was ringing, but of course, being Rob, he had to make it sound like a fluke, rather than good judgement! She turned round and her gaze was cool. 'I guess we all get lucky some time—even me,' she said quietly, before continuing up the stairs.

He caught up with her on the half landing, seizing her arm and turning her round with a strength that sent her staggering.

'Don't you know an apology when you hear one?' he demanded.

Jenna steadied herself by grasping the banister. 'Of course! Don't we all?' she asked, giving him glare for glare.

'And?'

She was heartily sick of all the hostility, but surely he didn't expect her to melt because he'd offered her a glass of sherry and a half-hearted compliment?

'You mentioned an apology,' she said a trifle unsteadily, 'but I think I can be forgiven for not understanding that was what you intended.'

'You do like your pound of flesh,' he said bitterly.

'No, Doctor. All I want is to be treated with—with the respect and consideration due to a colleague. Is that too much to ask?'

He stared at her for what felt like hours, his expression unreadable. Then at last he said gruffly, 'No, of course it's not. It's the way it should be. I've been treating you like a student. I'm—sorry.'

'I have to know this,' she said earnestly, green eyes wide with appeal. 'Would you have treated a male colleague the same way?'

'Probably,' he said grudgingly, after another lengthy pause.

Jenna didn't believe him. 'You don't like women doctors, do you?' she challenged. 'If I were a man, I could be just average and that'd be all right. But I'm a woman, so I have to be perfect to pass muster. And God knows I'm far from perfect, so—so. . .' Jenna had run out of steam. This had been the perfect chance to patch things up, but between his pride and her over-sensitivity, they'd blown it. 'I suppose I'll have to stay the probationary three months,' she sighed. 'I don't see any way round that.'

'Neither do I,' he agreed. 'But let's at least get one thing straight. I've got nothing at all against women doctors—if they're competent. My mother was a doctor.'

'She was? I didn't know that.'

'Why should you? You've only been here eighteen days.'

'It seems much longer than that.'

'To me as well,' he insisted. 'But we've just got to try and get along.'

'Yes,' Jenna agreed, but doubtfully. 'It might help if only we knew why we don't. It's ridiculous really. Two mature, reasonably intelligent people——'

'Oh, for God's sake!' he exploded. 'I know exactly why we don't get on! You took an instant dislike to me—it's as simple as that. And all because I didn't fawn all over you as my father did, preferring to reserve judgement and suss you out first. I've admitted as much—*and* apologised—but can you accept it? *No*! You have to go rabbiting on like a ruddy trick cyclist. Women!' With which scornful outburst, he bounded away down the stairs and into the sitting-room, slamming the door behind him with a force that shook the solid old house.

CHAPTER FOUR

FOR the next week or so, Jenna avoided Rob as much as possible. It wasn't difficult, because he was dodging her with equal determination. Basic exchanges at meals, strict formality in professional discussions and in her spare time Jenna took walks, went out with Nick or kept to her room.

Rob had definitely stopped breathing down her neck, though, and that was a great relief. It would have been nice to think that was because he now trusted her judgement—rather than being reluctant to offend further—but you couldn't have everything. It was clear that Dr William wasn't too happy with the situation, but, being wise, he said nothing.

At the same time, Belinda Duncan's father was saying a very great deal. In no time at all, it was all round Port Lindsay that clever little Dr Fielding had saved his daughter's life—and in a way that became more miraculous with every telling. Jenna tried hard to put the thing in perspective, but she was cast in the role of medical genius and that was that.

When the local paper came out on the Friday, they had given the story a whole page, plus a very unflattering photograph of Jenna getting out of her car, eyes shut and teeth bared in the smile they'd demanded. She was also showing a good deal more of her shapely thighs than was dignified in a GP.

The paper was delivered to Harbour House at teatime. Dr William thought it was a shame that the photo didn't do Jenna justice, while she thought it was a blatant example of sex discrimination. 'They'd never publish that sort of picture of a man!' she exclaimed.

Rob said he thought she had a point. 'It could have been worse though. At least they didn't ask you to unbutton your blouse,' he added gloomily.

Good grief! Did he think she'd lifted her skirt to order, then? 'It must have got caught up on the seatbelt or something,' she insisted.

He raised an eyebrow in that irritating way he had. 'What your blouse?'

'No! My skirt. I'd no idea I was showing that much leg. I've a good mind to sue.'

Dr William said he could understand her annoyance, but it was probably best to let sleeping dogs lie.

Then Rob asked, Why worry, when before the week was out, the papers would be round the fish and chips or going up the chimneys in smoke?

'I think I'll send it to a jumble sale,' said Jenna, still pursuing her own train of thought.

'The *East Coast Mail*?'

'That ruddy skirt!'

Rob was telling her not to bother unless she was planning to get into the papers on regular basis, when there came a thunderous knocking on the front door.

Naturally they all thought there'd been an accident, but when they piled out into the hall, the grocer's boy was hoisting a large crate on to the table, under Mrs Cullen's orders. 'And this came with it,' she said, handing an envelope to Jenna.

Jenna read the card inside and went pink with pleasure. 'It's from the Duncans,' she announced. 'A small token of our gratitude. . .'

'Vintage champagne!' breathed Dr William respectfully, having already inspected the crate's contents.

'We'll have it with our supper,' Jenna decided recklessly.

'What—all of it? Remember that stuff is very potent,' Rob advised practically.

'No, just one or two bottles. We ought to make it last.'

'Thank goodness,' said Dr William, who was on call that weekend and had been afraid of missing the treat.

'It must be properly chilled,' she went on excitedly, 'but as I'm taking surgery I'll have to leave that to you.'

Dr William said that was more in Rob's line than his.

'But am I to be trusted?' wondered his son thoughtfully.

Jenna met his gaze full on for almost the first time since that awful quarrel on the stairs. 'In this,' she said deliberately, 'I am quite happy to defer to your superior knowledge.'

'The devil you are!' breathed Rob in a way that suggested she might not have heard the last of it.

Jenna felt quite elated now and wondered why. Could it be that his attention, no matter how critical, was better than no attention at all?

The first patient that evening was Miss Wilma Smith, whom Rob had dealt with so patiently that first surgery they'd shared almost three weeks ago. 'You thought that Dr Rob was on tonight,' assumed Jenna after exchanging good evenings and agreeing that the weather, like everything else, was going from bad to worse.

Miss Smith scratched the side of her nose with a thoughtful forefinger. 'Well, no,' she demurred. 'Seeing as how you made such a good job of the Duncan girl, I thought I'd see what you can do for me.'

She then folded her hands in her lap and looked at Jenna, waiting to be cured.

Jenna didn't feel quite up to that. 'You shouldn't believe all you read in the papers,' she began. 'All I did was send Belinda to hospital. It was Mr Fraser, the neurosurgeon, who treated her.'

'Which he couldn't have if you'd not guessed what was wrong and sent her,' returned Miss Smith confidently.

Jenna said that any doctor would have done what she did, given the same circumstances, so Miss Smith asked what all the fuss was about in that case?

'You tell me,' sighed Jenna, hurrying on to ask how she liked her new pills before the patient could tell her.

'They don't agree with me, Doctor. They make me feel all jumpy.'

Not at all the sort of side-effect usually associated with tranquillisers. Jenna bit back a smile and said soothingly, 'Give them time, Miss Smith. Drugs like these have a cumulative effect. Remember Dr Rob said it would be several weeks before you really feel the benefit.'

'And you agree with him?'

'I certainly do.'

'Then that'll be right, I reckon.' She took a breath. 'I'm also having morning sickness.'

Her age and her solitary lifestyle counted against the usual cause, so Jenna wrote a prescription for a mild antacid, which Wilma Smith received as reverently as if it were the Holy Grail. 'I have great faith in you, Doctor,' she proclaimed.

Splendid, but for how long? wondered Jenna as she re-stressed the need to keep taking the new pills regularly, thus giving them the chance to do their work.

'Was it a heavy surgery, Jenna?' asked Dr William

when she eventually joined father and son at the round pine table in the kitchen.

'So so—the usual mix of aches and pains. Except for a new patient who's only just moved here. Such a nice old man with severe intermittent claudication. I'm referring him to the vascular clinic for an urgent assessment.'

'Then you'd better exaggerate his symptoms if you really want him seen quickly,' advised Rob.

'Too true. When I phone them tomorrow morning, I shall hint at early signs of gangrene. I'd rather be written off as a poor observer than risk him losing a leg. If he's not heading for a femoral artery occlusion, then—but enough of shop talk. This chicken looks delicious.'

Farmer Duncan certainly knew a good champagne and they were all three in a mellow mood by the time Rob upended the second bottle over Jenna's glass. He and she had drunk most of it. His father, being on duty, had refused more than half a glass.

A call came in just as they returned to the sitting-room, so Jenna and Rob were left alone. He didn't switch on the overhead light, but stirred the fire into a blaze, saying that it and the fireside lamps were all the light needed for drinking brandy.

'Brandy! How reckless,' she said.

Rob produced a bottle of Courvoisier. 'You're not the only one around here with grateful patients,' he told her.

'So it seems.' Jenna took an appreciative sip. 'And talking of patients, I have to confess to acquiring one of yours.'

'Feel free,' he invited. 'I've more than enough. Who is it?'

'Wilma Smith.'

Rob lounged back in his favourite chair and stretched his long legs towards the fire. 'Then you're more than welcome,' he said with a chuckle. 'So what's the problem this week?'

'The new tranks are making her all jumpy.'

He laughed; the attractive laugh she hadn't heard since the night she saw him with Susan MacArthur. 'Well, they would, wouldn't they?' he asked. 'She never runs true to form. Anything else?'

Somehow, she didn't mind his questions any more, accepting now that his interest was in the patient and not in scoring points.

'Morning sickness.'

He laughed again. 'I hope you asked for a urine sample.'

'I must confess I didn't. Is that what you'd have done?'

'No, though she could just about be young enough. Poor Wilma!' He drank some brandy. 'It'd probably be the making of her.'

'What—having a baby?'

'Having a man,' said Rob.

'Providing he knew what he was doing,' said Jenna. And I really must be drunk, talking to him like this. 'An incompetent could do more harm than good to a woman of her temperament.' She giggled just as she was about to sip her brandy, blowing bubbles in the glass.

Rob hadn't taken his eyes off her for quite some time. 'If you're going to treat my good cognac with such scant respect, the least you can do is to tell me why,' he challenged.

Jenna rotated the big glass between her palms, enjoying the sight of the rich amber liquid swirling. 'It's not really a laughing matter,' she said eventually. 'Poor Wilma's troubles are almost certainly rooted in her loneliness—and there's precious little any doctor can do about that. But you know that already. You said so yourself after her last visit.'

'So not everything I've said to you has been—unacceptable, then,' he said testingly.

'Good heavens, no!' she exclaimed.

'I thought I'd blown it a moment ago, though.'

'When? How?'

'When I said that Wilma needed a man. The minute I'd said it, I expected you to blow up and call me a sexist pig, or something equally unflattering.'

'Out of context—who knows? But there was more than a grain of truth in it then.'

'I hope Nick is measuring up,' he said next.

'What on earth do you mean? Oh, yes—I see. . . Actually, I'm not looking for that sort of relationship just now,' she said earnestly. Suddenly, it seemed very important to make him understand.

'And what about Nick?'

'I don't know. . .' But she did. She'd only been out with him a few times, but the signs were there. 'He's not really my type,' she said defensively.

'Who is?' he asked idly, staring into his glass, as she had a moment or so before.

'Nobody—just now,' Jenna said quietly.

'So I *was* right. You were running away.'

'I don't know what you mean,' she protested, thinking, I should never have let this get so personal. It was the champagne and the brandy that was to blame. And the firelight—and Rob in this unusually mellow mood. . .

She was startled when he drew in his long legs and rose swiftly, easily, crossing the hearthrug and dropping down beside her on the couch. 'What else but desperation could bring a girl like you to a place like this?'

'I—I just needed a complete change. . .' She was acutely aware of his nearness. He was half turned towards her, his left leg flexed, with the knee just touching her thigh. His elbow was resting on the back of the couch and his hand could easily slip on to her shoulder if he let it. He smelt clean and fresh—and very male.

'Well, you've certainly got that,' he agreed. 'Do you think it will—effect the cure?'

He was too attractive and he was getting to her and he was practically engaged to a girl called Susan MacArthur. Jenna set her glass down clumsily and stumbled to her feet. She was trembling. 'I was going through a bad patch when everything seemed to be going wrong,' she admitted unsteadily. 'The sort of low we all hit some time or other. So what better than a change of scene? We doctors prescribe it all the time for our patients.' She tried a light laugh, but it came out more like a strangled sob.

Rob got up too, towering over her. 'Except that your change of scene was from the frying-pan to the fire. Poor wee Jenna!'

She looked up defiantly. 'Oh, come—don't let's exaggerate. You were naturally wary of your new assistant and I over-reacted. That's all.'

'True as far as it goes, but——' He paused as though wondering how to proceed. 'Your predecessor was a woman.'

'I'd heard that.'

'And what else has Nick told you?'

He'd guessed correctly there. 'That you frightened her away with your high standards.'

Rob laughed briefly. 'If that's the prevailing version, then I'm very relieved. In fact it was—quite different.'

'Are you saying. . .?' Jenna couldn't believe it. 'She

must have been absolutely brilliant to frighten you! No wonder you were so determined to keep me in my place.'

He smiled twistedly. 'She wasn't one tenth the doctor you are. If fact, she was about as mediocre as they come.'

'Then why. . .?'

'From the minute she was over the doorstep, she was after me,' he said. 'The black widow spider is nothing beside her. The night she came naked into my room and tried to climb into bed with me, I sent her packing. That's why I insisted we got a man next time. Only there weren't any takers.'

No wonder he was so relieved that the truth hadn't leaked out! His precious Susan would have had a fit. 'You can rest assured you've nothing to fear from me in that direction,' Jenna said firmly.

'Because you've also had an unfortunate experience and are off men for the time being.'

'Did I say that?'

'You didn't need to, Jenna.'

There was that in his eyes which was both exhilarating and confusing. She was misreading their expression; she had to be. There was Susan. 'I think we women sometimes forget that sexual harassment can be a two-way process,' she said desperately. 'I'm so glad you told me about that ghastly woman—it's cleared the air.'

'Has it?' he asked quietly.

'Of course! It also explains why Mrs Cullen has been so funny with me. We must make it plain to her that you've got me firmly under control. In my place,' she corrected, unsure whether that was actually an improvement.

'Have I?' he asked. 'I wasn't aware of it. Have another brandy.'

She covered her glass and moved away from him. 'Not unless you want to replace your wanton assistant with a drunk,' she laughed.

'I'm only trying to keep you mellow,' he said. 'Normally, you're as prickly as a hedgehog.'

'*Me*—prickly—I like that! You could teach a porcupine a thing or two.'

'We got off on the wrong foot,' he said.

'That is probably the understatement of the year,' Jenna told him, just as the phone rang. The private, not the surgery one. Being nearest, Jenna picked it up. 'Rob? What the hell do you think you're doing?' shrilled an angry female voice. It sobered Jenna up better than a cold shower.

She covered the mouthpiece and passed the thing to Rob. 'For you—your girlfriend, I imagine. And she sounds very angry.'

Rob frowned, cleared his throat and said awkwardly, 'Is anything wrong, Sue?'

She told him—at length and at such a pitch that she could probably be heard in the street outside. 'I was supposed to go over and take her out for a drink tonight,' he relayed unnecessarily when Susan had flung down her phone and almost certainly broken it.

'Oh, dear,' said Jenna. 'Perhaps you'd better——'

'Go round now? It's nearly midnight.'

'*Is* it? Where has the evening gone?'

'Time flies when you're having—an important and air-clearing discussion,' he said deliberately.

'I don't think she'll take that for an excuse,' said Jenna. 'I wouldn't. And heavens, you're not the only one in trouble. I sort of half promised to meet Nick at the Lobster Pot.'

'But he didn't ring,'

'If he had, you might have avoided offending your—um, er. . .' She only had Nick's word for it that Rob and Susan were more or less engaged.

'Which is of course far more important than ironing out *our* differences.'

What was he suggesting? '*As* important, anyway, surely,' she insisted. 'Things have to be kept in proportion.'

'How very sensible you are,' Rob said tonelessly. 'It makes me wonder how you let things get to the point of needing a change of scene at all!' He yawned elaborately before saying, 'I'm for bed now. Would you mind putting the fireguard in place before you go up?'

'Not at all—*Doctor*,' breathed Jenna as the door shut behind him. What a puzzle he was! What the hell had come over him just then? They'd been getting on so well before Susan rang. Naturally, forgetting his promise had annoyed him, but there was more to it than that. What could it be?

I've drunk far too much tonight, she decided. My brain's quite fuddled. The best thing I can do is go to bed myself and sleep it off.

'Dr Rob has had his breakfast and gone out on an urgent message,' explained Mrs Cullen, slapping a bowl of porridge down in front of Jenna.

To the MacArthurs' farm, of course, anxious to make his peace as soon as possible. She found such haste depressing and wondered why, until she thought it must be because it reminded her of the way it always was with her and Jake. She, ever eager to apologise, even when it wasn't her fault. Was Rob as besotted with Susan as she had been with Jake? Now if only she could be quite clear in her mind about all that was said last night—

'You're not eating your porridge,' said Mrs Cullen severely. 'Are ye not feeling well?'

'I'm fine, thank you.' Jenna picked up her spoon. 'I suppose Dr William has had his breakfast,' she went on, purely for something to say.

Mrs Cullen looked sorrowful. 'He'll be lucky if he gets any at all today. He was called out again at three and I had to wake him about ten minutes since.'

'Oh, I do wish you hadn't, cried Jenna. 'I can easily take surgery.'

'I'll away up and tell him to stay in his bed, then.' She strode over to the door.

Not so much as a smile, thought Jenna gloomily. I'll never make the grade with her. Of course I'm doing it for William, not her. All the same—

He came in, still in pyjamas and dressing-gown and with his sparse grey hair standing up like windblown straw. 'You're not taking surgery, Jenna,' he said firmly, then spoiling it with a yawn, quickly stifled.

'Oh, yes, I am,' she insisted. 'I've nothing else to do and it's far too wet to go for a walk.'

'This is my weekend on,' he returned doggedly.

'And I'm the one who's dressed and ready. Anyway, I'm only paying back a favour. You did the same for me after I had that frantic night on call.'

He had to admit that, so Jenna said there it was then and hurried off to open the shop before he could think of another objection.

Rob didn't come back until she was seeing the last patient. He opened the surgery door and stared. 'Is my father ill?' he asked anxiously.

'No, he's fine, Doctor. We swapped duties, that's all.' Jenna wasn't going into details in front of Mrs Kerr, chronic asthmatic and notorious gossip.

'I only want a quick glance at Davidson's *Principles*,' said Rob, reaching into the bookcase behind her. He then exchanged a few words with Mrs Kerr, smiled at Jenna again and went out.

'Dr William's never been the same since Dr Margaret died,' volunteered Mrs Kerr while Jenna was writing a repeat prescription for her water pills, as she called them.

'It must have been a great blow,' Jenna agreed neutrally.

'Aye, it was! She was gey popular and we were all very worried about who we'd get instead.' That wasn't quite what Jenna had meant but she let it pass. 'And then Dr Rob came home, so that was all right.'

'I'm sure it was.'

'Aye, though nobody expected him to stay.'

Jenna managed not to ask the leading question she was bursting to put.

'Well, I mean to say! When he had the Professor's ear and all—or so Senga Shaw's girl says. The one that's a secretary in yon big hospital in Dundee. Are you quite sure I still need the water pills, Doctor?'

Jenna dragged her mind away from contemplation of Rob's sacrificed glories to explain once more the importance of taking diuretics when you were also taking steroids. 'I know it's a bore, and one more thing to remember, but you wouldn't want your legs to swell up, now would you, Mrs Kerr?' Not with those short skirts and high heels, you wouldn't!

Mrs Kerr said no, she certainly would not and went away, leaving Jenna to digest what she'd heard. Rob may or may not have intended all along to make general practice his life's work, but it hadn't been

Hobson's choice. She wasn't surprised. He was a brilliant diagnostician. That, and his strong personality and winning way with patients, would have guaranteed favourable notice from senior consultants. She wondered if he ever regretted his choice.

Dr William wandered in while Jenna was tidying the desk. He looked rested and she guessed he'd spent most of the morning sleeping. 'Just checking that you're not sneaking off to do the calls,' he said with a mock frown.

'If I sneak anywhere, it'll be upstairs to wash my hair,' she said.

'No further?' he queried. 'You've not been away anywhere since you came.'

'I know. My home is in Yorkshire as you know and that'd be rather far, just for a weekend.'

'Yes, I suppose it would. You must have some friends in Edinburgh, though. How long were you there?'

'A year and a bit—doing the GP course. It was very concentrated though and I didn't get much chance to make friends. Are there many calls, Dr William, dear?'

'Only three so far. See you at lunchtime, then, Jenna.' He never probed, at least not when she put up the shutters.

She remained at the desk, thinking. Edinburgh. Such a lovely city, but it was true she hadn't had much social life. Not between work and swotting and pampering Jake and worrying herself sick about what he was doing when he wasn't with her. God, what a fool she'd been all those years!

'There's a letter for you, Doctor,' said Mrs Cullen when Jenna went through to the house. 'It came with the second post,' she added as though somehow, that made it more important.

Jenna took it, recognised Jake's writing with a little

jolt and stuffed it in the pocket of her skirt. 'Thanks,' she said casually, loath to satisfy the housekeeper's curiosity. Her first instinct was to tear it up unread, but later, in her room, she opened it. The poignant picture of suffering he had painted would have wrung her heart once. Now her reaction was largely irritation—and that mostly with herself for playing the doormat for so long. She tore the letter into tiny fragments before she'd finished it and threw them in the waste-paper basket.

When she went down to lunch, Rob was already there. He half rose from the table as she entered. 'Thank you for doing surgery this morning, Jenna,' he said warmly. 'I'm really grateful.'

'No need to thank me—I was glad to do it. I hadn't anything to do this morning.'

'And—this afternoon?'

'I had thought of tackling Lindsay Law now it's stopped raining, but if there's anything—some visits perhaps—I'm quite willing.'

'No—nothing like that. Things are quiet and Dad insists he can cope after his extra sleep. Thanks to you.'

'Stop it! All this praise is very blush-making,' she claimed.

He looked at her, his blue eyes thoughtful. 'I imagine it must be. Getting "the respect and consideration due to a colleague" instead of——'

'Rob, please don't! I was at fault too. Didn't I admit that last night?'

He flashed her a brief, disturbing grin. 'Last night, we were both rather well oiled. I wasn't sure you'd remember—anything that was said.'

'I remember that.' I also remember why the evening ended the way it did! Had Susan forgiven him yet? 'You went out very early this morning,' she hinted gently.

'A house call which wasn't as urgent as it sounded.

I wanted to save Dad, when he'd been out twice already.'

So it hadn't been an anxious lover's dash to put things right after all! 'And you praised *me* for helping out,' she said.

'Well, he is more my concern than yours.'

'I know that, but don't we both think he should be persuaded to cut down a bit? Perhaps we could work out a new timetable.'

'I'd appreciate that—if and when we can find the time.'

'No time like the present,' she volunteered.

Rob quartered an apple and bit into it thoughtfully. 'Except that your friend Nick—who isn't really your type—will probably be here any minute to carry you off for that walk.'

'Nick's gone to Edinburgh for the Rugby International and won't be back until tomorrow.' And he wasn't awfully pleased when I said I wouldn't go with him.

'Is that so? So if I were to go with you—and I need the exercise—we could map out a new routine as we went.' He sat back as though expecting a blasting refusal.

'And no time wasted. What a brilliant idea,' Jenna said firmly.

They took Rob's car the four miles to the foot of the hill and the sun was breaking through the clouds when they backed on to the grass verge which did duty as a car park at the end of the road. At fifteen hundred feet, rugged Lindsay Law was the highest hill for miles around and it dominated the surrounding farmland.

'You're a serious walker,' realised Jenna, watching Rob exchange his leather loafers for thick socks and tough boots. His tweed jacket followed the loafers into the boot, to be replaced by a waxed green three-quarter coat.

'When you live in a place like Port Lindsay, you either walk or sail, according to the time of the year,' he returned. 'There's precious little else to do.'

'But you love the place.' It was one of the first things she'd noticed about him.

'It's my home,' he said simply, holding out a hand to help her over the stile that guarded the path to the hill.

Jenna accepted, although she didn't need help. His hand was dry, warm and firm; rather like the man himself. Susan MacArthur was lucky in her man. There was a moment's disappointment when Rob let go of her hand—and that was silly, whichever way you looked at it. He scorned the step himself and vaulted lightly over.

'Impressive stuff,' declared Jenna.

'Showing off,' he said. 'And grateful to find I can still manage it at thirty-three!'

She'd thought he was older, and said so.

'Because I'm so severe and bad-tempered?'

'Because you're so serious and dedicated. One doesn't see too much of that these days—more's the pity.'

'Then how come a mere babe like you goes in for it?'

'This mere babe will soon be a sober twenty-eight,' she remembered with slight shock. All those precious years, wasted on a man like Jake. . .

'But she'd easily pass for sweet sixteen on a grey day in Port Lindsay,' he sang in a passable baritone and clever parody of Gilbert and Sullivan.

Jenna chuckled delightedly. 'Oh, Rob, you're so amusing!'

'Think so?' he asked with a grin. 'Then things *are* looking up. Come on—race you to the top.'

It wasn't exactly a race, more of a scramble. The path was steep and quite tricky in parts, and Jenna was glad of the strong arm extended so often to haul her over the worst bits. The wind at the top was fierce and biting and they huddled in the lee of the ridge to get their breath back. There wasn't much shelter, so it was a close huddle. Susan would definitely not have approved.

'I wonder if I'd have made it on my own?' mused Jenna from under Rob's Barbour jacket, which he'd unzipped and opened out to envelop them both.

'I expect so,' he said. 'You're a very determined little thing.'

'All the same, I think I would've got blown away without my anchorman.'

'Or frozen to death without his jacket. There's no warmth in that anorak thing you're wearing.'

'But it says "windproof" on the label. Look!'

'It also says "made in Hong Kong", and that's a lot nearer the equator than we are.'

'I wonder if I'll ever get the better of an argument with you?' wondered Jenna.

'Is it necessary that you should?'

'Not now, not this minute—no. Rob. . .'

'Yes, Jenna?'

A sudden vicious flurry of wind-driven hail stung their faces, making them flinch. 'I can think of better places than this for a chat,' said Rob. Then with an exclamation of remembrance, he pulled a bright red cagoul from the capacious packet of his coat and put it on Jenna, over her own gear. It was a bit on the big side, but it was undoubtedly a woman's. Susan's, of course. Then he seized Jenna's hand and towed her down the hill on the lee side.

The going was even more tricky now than the ascent

had been, but at least here the hill provided some protection from the wind and driving rain.

They seemed to be making for a ruined cottage on a gentler slope about halfway down. 'What a place to build a house,' breathed Jenna when they finally gained its shelter.

'No accounting for taste,' agreed Rob. 'But the view is great. When you can see it, that is.'

'And when is that?' Jenna wondered with a sigh. 'I've been here nearly a month and we've only had four decent days.'

'The weather is particularly bad this year—and remember it's only early March.'

'I've picked primroses in March—in England.'

'Oh, England!' said Rob scornfully, taking off his coat and giving it a good shake to get rid of the surface water.

Jenna wasn't going down that road. She wanted to go on being friends with Rob too much to risk a quarrel.

'But then it is further south,' she allowed. 'Rob—about your father. We were going to plan how we could take over more of his work.'

'That's right—so we were, Pixie.'

Had he really forgotten why they'd come out together? But the reason why he'd called her Pixie was more pressing a question. She asked it.

'Because that's how you look with that waterproof thing almost down to your knees and the hood—and your hair curling all round your face. And your funny little turned-up nose. . .' He pulled a handkerchief from his pocket and gently mopped her wet cheeks. 'And you're all wet too. A water pixie. . .'

But it wasn't all rain. Some of the drops were foolish tears, welling up in response to the unexpected tenderness in his voice. Not once in the five stormy years of their affair had she had such gentleness from Jake.

'Jenna—little one. . .' When he kissed her, his kisses too were soft and gentle. At first. They soon grew more urgent, compelling a response. It was quite wonderful. It was also very confusing.

But Jenna wasn't the only one surprised and in doubt. Rob released her clumsily, his expression a mixture of wonder and embarassment. 'Jenna—I'm so sorry. I shouldn't have done that. I don't know what I could have been thinking of. . .'

Jenna swallowed her disappointment. 'Just—one of those things, I guess. It—doesn't matter.' And I won't broadcast it. Susan will never get to know.

'Do you really mean that?'

He wanted reassurance. Of course. Didn't they always. 'Quite sure.'

'I should have remembered. What you said last night about not wanting anything—like that. . .'

Men were so good at this; using something you'd said for an excuse, when they were feeling guilty about going behind another woman's back. Silly to have supposed Rob wasn't like the rest. 'Forget it,' she said brusquely. 'I have. And in case you hadn't noticed, it's stopped raining.'

'You're a wonderful—a really exceptional girl, Jenna. I mean that.'

Of course he did! He'd probably been afraid that she would cling, even babble on about love and generally complicate things, instead of backing off and letting him off the hook the way she had.

'That's nice,' she said in a cracked, brittle little voice. 'Just you go on believing that—and I'll look forward to a wonderful report when I leave Port Lindsay.'

CHAPTER FIVE

Rob drove fast back to Port Lindsay, his profile stern and his eyes only for the road. When, tired of the stiff and uncomfortable silence, Jenna ventured to point out a break in the clouds, he only said, 'Too late.' Chilling.

Jenna shrank into Susan's cagoul and wondered why her life had to be so complicated. A rogue gene perhaps. That seemed to be the explanation for so many physical ailments these days. Why not for emotional problems as well? She shivered and Rob noticed. 'You'd better have a hot bath as soon as we get in,' he decided. 'And if you intend to make a habit of long walks, go to Dundee on your next half-day and buy yourself some warmer gear. Talk to Meg. She has a cousin who runs a country-sports shop there.'

'You're very practical,' she told him in a small voice.

'That goes with the job. Or should do,' he added woodenly. Was he back to criticising her again, then? If so, it was too much.

They parted in the hall of Harbour House without another word. Jenna hung the borrowed cagoul on the hallstand and went up to her room. Her clothes were almost dry now from the heat of the car, but she was still cold. It went against the grain to obey Rob and take a bath, so she showered instead. Then she put on fresh undies, light trousers and a baggy sweater. No make-up, and with her blonde hair clinging damply to her temples and curling in the nape of her graceful neck she went downstairs, meaning to make herself a mug of tea.

The sitting-room door was ajar and Rob called out to her. She went, reluctantly. He was kneeling on the hearthrug and making toast at the fire. He too had changed, into jeans and a checked Viyella shirt, open at the neck and with the sleeves rolled up. 'The tea's freshly made. Help yourself,' he said without looking round.

It would have been rude and pointless to refuse. 'Thank you,' said Jenna. And then, 'That toast smells good,' which it did. She couldn't remember the last time she'd tasted real toast, made in the old-fashioned way.

He half turned then, holding the fork towards her at arm's length. 'Help yourself,' he said again.

'No—honestly. I didn't mean——'

'Don't be silly. It'll only take a minute to do some more.'

'All right, then, thank you.' She paused. 'I suppose William is out on a call.'

'No, away to see his friend the minister. I'll deal with anything that crops up between now and eight.'

She almost asked him why eight before realising she already knew the answer. On Saturdays, he always went out with Susan. 'I'm not going out, so I could take over,' she offered, hoping to improve things between them.

'If he'll let you,' Rob returned shortly. 'Now butter your toast. It's not the same when it's cold.'

Jenna knelt too, on the other side of the table from Rob. The tension in the room was almost tangible and her hand trembled as she spread the butter. She thought she knew why he was so ill at ease. It was quite common for a man to be attracted to another woman, while already in a steady relationship. Jake was living proof of that. But only a decent man would feel guilty about it.

'Jam?' he offered and she started, flushing foolishly—a mass of jumbled emotions herself.

'What sort?' she asked, as if it mattered.

He had to look at the label. 'Rhubarb and ginger.'

'My favourite.'

'Mine too. Something else in common,' he said gloomily.

'Like what?'

'Medicine. What else?'

What else indeed? 'Yes—of course. . .'

'You're still embarrassed!' he burst out. 'Damn it—I said I was sorry!'

'And I told you to forget it. Let's leave it there!'

'If that's—really what you want. . .'

What was he doing? Trying to make out the choice was all hers? How dared he? She wasn't the one with a prior commitment! 'Men!' fumed Jenna, now at the end of her tether. 'You're all the same. I'm going upstairs!'

She stayed there until she heard the front door closing and made sure it was Rob going out by watching him cross the road to his car and then drive away. William hadn't come back, so she went to the surgery to check for any recorded messages. None. She switched the phone through to her room and went back upstairs. On the way, she glanced at the hallstand. The red cagoul had gone.

On Monday, Rob took morning surgery and when Jenna went to get her list of calls, he handed her a typewritten sheet. 'You'll see that I've divided the on-call between us. I hope that meets with your approval.'

His tone was even and his manner quiet, with none of the awkwardness that had marred their last encounter.

'Of course. It's the obvious thing.' And also made sure that they were never off duty together again!

'You're quite sure you don't mind the extra work?'

'You didn't need to ask that, Rob,' Jenna said reproachfully.

'No—I didn't. I'm sorry.'

'What did William say?'

'He was furious. Said I was trying to pension him off.'

'Shall I tell him it was a joint decision?'

'Thank you, that should help.' He swallowed visibly, the calm veneer cracking for a second. 'He thinks the world of you.'

'I'm glad that somebody does,' retorted Jenna flatly, before going out and shutting the door firmly.

It was the first time they'd talked since Saturday. Nick had changed his mind about staying the night in Edinburgh after the match and had come round to carry Jenna off right after breakfast yesterday. They had gone for a long drive through the glens of Angus. For once the weather was fine and they'd gone for a walk, laughing and talking non-stop. On the way home, he kissed her. Quite a lot. Skilfully and with no undertones of emotion—or guilt. Just sex attraction, pure and simple. If sex could ever be said to be just that.

Only Jenna wasn't in the mood. Nick had said not to worry, he could wait, but not too long. She hadn't told him that, the way she was feeling, she'd never be in the mood again.

Jenna was taking evening surgery; the usual assortment of repeat prescriptions, minor but debilitating ailments like flu which required sick notes, and lastly—or so she thought—a young fisherman with a very nasty gash on his leg which needed a lot of tidying up and some careful stitching. She'd done all that, washed her hands, given him an anti-tetanus injection and was reaching for the sick notes when he said, 'Ye can forget that, Doctor. I work for myself.'

'You can't work with an injury like that,' she said flatly. 'If that leg's not rested for at least five days, it won't heal properly—even with the stitching.'

'Tell that to the Man from the Ministry,' he said satirically. 'After all the storms, the forecast is good now and if I rest for five days I'll only have had four days' fishing this month. By the end of the week, it'll be tie-up time.' The compulsory time in harbour every month, designed to conserve fish stocks.

'Those fixed days are a damn silly rule that ought to be waived when the weather's bad,' fumed Jenna, who was now *au fait* and fully sympathetic with the fishermen's problems.

'You tell that to the politicians—and remind them they get paid every day—whatever.'

'So do I,' she reminded him.

'Aye—but you earn it, which is more than ye can say for the Westminster Windbag Society. What wouldn't I give to get them out to sea in a force ten. . .' His eyes gleamed.

'And a Saturday night in a city hospital's casualty department would open their eyes as well,' said Jenna, in the same heartfelt tones. 'Look, if you're absolutely determined to go to sea, then I'll give you a shot of penicillin and put a light plaster cast on that leg. It ought to be firm enough by morning.'

'That's the stuff, Doctor. Ye're getting more like Dr Rob every day,' he approved.

Jenna was grateful for his confidence. She was growing very attached to the hardy, energetic folk of Port Lindsay, but with things so fraught between her and Rob, how much longer could she stay here?

She was tidying the desk when Meg came in. 'There's one more, Doctor. You've not been that busy the night, and she did ask for you specially. I hope you don't mind. . .' She handed Jenna a file, then stepped aside. It was Mrs Shelagh Donaldson, née MacArthur, who came in.

When women asked specifically for a woman doctor, it often meant that they had a gynaecological problem, but, having taken off her coat, Shelagh Donaldson removed her sweater. 'It's my neck, Dr Fielding,' she explained. 'I've had trouble with it before, but it's actually keeping me awake at night this time.'

Jenna asked the obvious question first. 'Have you injured it at any time? A car accident perhaps?'

'No, nothing like that. It just come and goes. . .'

Jenna went through the routine, testing movements, palpating the neck and shoulder muscles and asking about changes in sensation such as tingling, numbness and patterns of pain. In the end she said, 'In the absence of any likelier cause, you've probably got some osteo-arthritic changes in your neck joints. That's something we all get to a greater or lesser degree after our mid-twenties. Have you had this particular bout long?'

'About a month.'

'I see. Well, I can give you something for the pain, but in the long run, physiotherapy is probably your best bet. However, that means seeing a hospital consultant and there's quite a waiting list.'

'I have a physio friend in private practice in Dundee,' said Shelagh. 'And before you ask, she is properly qualified; worked at the Royal Infirmary there before she married.'

'Perfect. I'll give you a note for her,' said Jenna, reaching for a sheet of paper. 'Right, there you are then, Mrs Donaldson. A note for your friend and a prescription for distalgesic. Let me know how you progress, won't you?'

'Of course.' Shelagh tucked the papers away in her bag and stood up, but made no move to leave. 'God, this is difficult!' she burst out at last. 'And I'd thought I could just walk in and say it. . .'

She must have a gynae problem after all. 'Sit down again, and take all the time you want,' Jenna invited gently. 'And there's absolutely no need for any embarrassment.' She relaxed back in her chair, waiting to be told what was wrong. A pelvic infection, an unwanted pregnancy. . .

'The town is right about you,' said Susan's sister. 'You *are* a good doctor. But why the hell did you have to come *here*?'

Jenna stared at her in astonishment, shaken out of her calm professional manner by the woman's vehemence. 'You'll have to explain, she said crisply.

'It would be easier if you weren't so damned nice!' She was now pacing restlessly about. 'I—have a sister,' she said. 'And we're very close.'

Good grief, she's going to warn me off, realised Jenna at last. But what makes her think she needs to? She took a deep breath and said, 'That's not so unusual. Especially if there's not a big age difference.'

'Just eighteen months. We both fell in love with the same man—and I got him. Of course I felt dreadful about that, but turning him down would only have made three people miserable. So you can imagine how delighted I was when Rob Strachan came home and they started going out. They'd always been good friends and soon became inseparable. They were taking their time, though, and I thought that was just because they wanted to be sure. Then recently, he seemed to be cooling off—and Susan is devastated. *Now* do you understand?'

Jenna thought she did, but she fought to keep her elation out of her voice and her expression as she said, 'I understand your concern for your sister, but how am I supposed to fit into all this?'

'When a man cools off for no apparent reason, it usually means he's seeing somebody else. And who can it be but you? Especially as it's only since you came!' She darted up to the desk, leaning forward and staring pleadingly at Jenna. 'You've got Nick Lawson dangling after you, so why can't you leave Rob for my sister? I don't think she could take another rejection.'

What she's really doing is asking me to do what she wouldn't do herself, thought Jenna, but she would be keeping this impersonal. 'If Rob really loves your sister, then she's got nothing to fear. If he doesn't, then she'll lose him anyway—sooner or later—to somebody. That's life, I'm afraid.'

'It's easy to see *you've* always got what you wanted,' flared Shelagh.

'That's not true. I learned that particular lesson the hard way. Just as your sister did when you married the man she loved.'

Susan's sister looked at Jenna for a long, assessing moment. 'They're also saying that you're very clever, Dr Fielding. It seems they're right about that too. I've done no good at all by coming here, have I?' Then she picked up her bag and stormed out. Seconds later, the outside door banged shut.

Jenna went on sitting there and thinking. That

extraordinary visit had been very revealing. Rob was obviously fond of Susan MacArthur but he wasn't in love with her, whatever people thought. And if he wasn't in love with her, then those bittersweet moments in the ruined cottage on the hill—as well as his stumbling explanations later—took on quite a different meaning. Jenna was happier than she'd been for weeks; no, for years.

She hurried through to the house, eager to see Rob. She'd no idea what she would say to him, but surely the right words would come.

Only William and the housekeeper were in the kitchen. 'Is Rob out on a call, then?' asked Jenna as she took her place at the table.

'Not as far as I know,' his father answered. 'Anyway, now that I'm declared an invalid, I understood that you were on call tonight.' He sounded aggrieved.

'Oh, William!' Jenna stretched out an impulsive hand towards him. 'All we're trying to do is to see that you get enough sleep and a regular routine. If one of us was a bit under the weather, you'd do exactly the same. You know you would.'

'That's true,' said Mrs Cullen unexpectedly. Jenna had never expected support from that quarter.

'And you wouldn't be on tonight anyway—not after your weekend on—'

'When you and Rob did as much work as I did. Oh, all right! I know when I'm licked. Are you going to put me to bed with a cup of Horlicks at half-past nine?'

'No, you may stay up for the ten o'clock news,' laughed Jenna. 'But only if you're very good.'

Before Rob came home, Jenna was called out to treat a boy with an acute asthmatic attack and when she got back, Rob had gone to bed.

Next morning, roles were reversed. Rob was already

away to a suspected heart attack when Jenna went down to breakfast, and he didn't return before she set out on her calls.

William was taking surgery that morning. At least, that was the plan. When Jenna went back to base mid-morning because she'd been given the wrong notes for one of her patients, she found a small crowd gossiping quietly on the pavement outside Harbour House. And in the crowded waiting-room was a damp-eyed Meg.

Full of dread, she hurried along to the consulting-room. Rob had just finished binding up the cut fingers of a tough-looking little boy. When he saw Jenna, he gave a few final words of advice to his mother, then hurried them out before calling to Meg to hold the next one until he buzzed. Then he went back to Jenna.

'Your father. . .' she began fearfully.

'A myocardial infarct—but not too severe, thank God. He was taken off to hospital about ten minutes ago.'

'If only I'd come back sooner, you could have gone with him,' she sighed.

'You don't usually come back at all until lunch time.'

'There was something. . .' She'd almost forgotten what in her anxiety. 'You must let me finish surgery,' she begged. 'Then you can to go the hospital.'

'But what about all the calls, Jenna?' That he'd even asked showed he was tempted.

'There aren't too many today and I've seen the new ones already. The repeats could be left if necessary. I can easily get through yours in time for evening surgery.'

'Thanks, but I've got a couple of specials this afternoon, so——'

'Couldn't I see them for you tomorrow afternoon?'

'Tomorrow is your half-day.'

'Oh, damn that! This is an emergency.'

'But, Jenna—'

'Now listen to me! If we were running a corner shop instead of a medical practice, you wouldn't hesitate. William needs you, Rob!'

'Bless you, Jenna,' he said huskily. 'I'll not forget this.' She thought he was going to kiss her and leaned forward, but he only touched her lightly on the cheek and went away.

There were fewer patients waiting than Jenna had thought. Some of the folk in the waiting-room were merely passers-by who had looked in to get the latest news of their beloved Dr William. News travelled fast in Port Lindsay.

'You'll have a coffee before you go out again, Doctor,' Meg urged.

'OK—thanks. Just a quickie while I look something out.' Ugh! Meg hadn't sugared the coffee. She'll be upset, if I say anything, though. 'Would you cancel Dr Rob's afternoon patients, please, Meg, and ask them to come and see me tomorrow instead?'

'But, Doctor, Wednesday's your—'

'Not this week—we're in crisis. And let Mrs Cullen know I'll be a bit late for lunch, will you?' Then she could squeeze in those four calls that were practically on their doorstep. . .

Home for a late lunch and a lecture from Mrs Cullen about not running herself into the ground like Dr William. She'd barely had time to imagine she'd gained favour at last when the housekeeper added, 'That would make things too difficult for Dr Rob.'

'I'm a bit younger than Dr William and I thrive on hard work,' insisted Jenna.

Mrs Cullen conceded both points and said she might

just make scones for tea. Jenna pretended she hadn't heard that. With Rob's most urgent calls to make, plus another that had just come in, she'd be hard put to it to get back in time for evening surgery.

When Jenna eventually returned to Harbour House ten minutes late, Rob's car was in its accustomed place in the quayside park. Did that mean good or bad news about William?'

Rob was in the consulting-room with the first patient. 'Sorry I'm late. . .' she was beginning when he looked up and smiled warmly. Excusing himself to the patient, he joined Jenna in the passage. 'I'm doing surgery tonight,' he said firmly.

'But—'

'No buts, please. If you can't find anything else to do, then away and put your feet up.'

'Not until you've told me how William is.'

'The offical view is "comfortable". The ECG showed a myocardial infarct of moderate severity and they've got him in Coronary Care with all the usual monitoring.'

'Thank God you were here when it happened,' she breathed. 'So he's definitely not in danger, then?'

'Not if he behaves himself. Where's your objectivity, Jenna?' he asked gently.

'I'm so fond of him,' she said and it was true.

'That's mutual,' he told her. 'And I'm beginning to feel excluded. Now will you please go and take a break? I don't want two lame ducks on my hands.'

Jenna did as she was told. Rob was so much more relaxed tonight that he had to be satisfied with his father's condition.

Meg caught Jenna before she could go into the house. 'Oh, Dr Jenna, there's been such a nasty accident at the crossroads.'

That was the first time she'd raised Jenna to equal status with the others, but Jenna was too worried to notice. 'Where exactly, Meg? Any details?' She was picturing cars in a pile-up.

'You know—that holiday camp place at the top of the hill. The owner's wee boy has chopped off his arm.'

'I'm away,' snapped Jenna, galvanised into action again. She'd got her bearings now and Meg's garbled account had been more than enough to indicate dire emergency. Speeding up the long hill out of town and passing Nick's flat without a thought. None of the chalets and caravans were occupied at this time of the year, so it was easy to locate the owner's by the smoke curling up from the chimney. Jenna parked and pushed her way through an agitated crowd of relatives.

The boy was lying on the kitchen floor. He was chalk-white and scarcely breathing. Regardless of the great pool of blood around him, Jenna dropped to her knees. The child was steadily bleeding to death as the brachial artery pumped out his life blood. Slower than one would have expected, though. This must have been going on some time. Jenna tore off her scarf and tied it round his arm above the terrible wound. 'That wooden spoon, quickly—*quickly*!'

The tourniquet working, the flow stopped ominously soon. He must have lost far too much blood. She had to get him to hospital fast. In record time, Jenna had set up a drip, while sending folk scurrying round for blankets. Then she reached up and snatched a pillow-case off the overhead airer and wrapped it round the arm.

'Are ye no' going to dress his arm, Doctor?' asked an ancient grannie disapprovingly.

'They'll fix it at the hospital.' Jenna scooped up the boy and put him with his mother in the back of her car, with the child well bundled up in blankets to preserve what remained of his body heat. The nearest relative was dragooned into the front seat, given the drip bottle to hold and warned to keep it as high as possible on pain of everything that was awful.

Driving to the hospital at breakneck speed on unfamiliar roads and in a light mist was scary. Fortunately there was little traffic.

Arriving at Casualty and marching straight into the nearest empty treatment-room, Jenna was promptly accosted by an elderly sister, asking furious questions.

'No, I don't know his Christian name and no, I didn't take his blood-pressure. Why the hell would I bother when he'd lost enough blood for an elephant?' She grabbed a white-coated man. 'Are you the duty surgeon? Then get in there at once! My patient has all but bled to death.' If he hadn't already. . .

At last, satisfied that she'd done all she could, Jenna sank on to the nearest chair and closed her eyes.

'Have you checked in?' asked a bright cheerful young voice.

Jenna opened her eyes and stared at a very young student nurse. 'There's nothing wrong with me. I'm the GP who brought in the boy. . .' She pointed to the cubicle.

'Oh, *that* doctor. Gosh! You didn't half put Sister in her place. She's been asking for it for years and everybody's thrilled. Would you like me to get you a nice strong coffee and a chocolate biscuit, Doctor?'

'I'd love both, but first, how is my patient?'

'They're pumping in the plasma as fast as they dare, but it's touch and go. His BP's almost too low to register. Mr Savage says he'd be a goner for sure, but for you. God, I'd love to be a doctor, but I only got one A level. . .'

'A good nurse is worth five bad doctors,' said Jenna.

'Do you really think so? How marvellous! I'll go and get your coffee.' She sped away leaving Jenna feeling better than if she'd had a stiff dram.

The coffee, which was filtered and not out of the machine in the waiting-room, perked Jenna up some more and she decided to find Coronary Care and check up on William while she was here.

'Casualty is on the ground floor, near the main entrance. I can't think how you missed it,' said the nurse-in-charge when she saw Jenna's blood-stained clothing.

Jenna began to laugh. 'No wonder you thought I was a casualty! Actually I've just brought in one of our patients who was too severely injured to wait for an ambulance. I'm Dr Fielding from the Port Lindsay practice.'

'What a day you're having—what with your partner and all! I suppose you'd like to see Dr Strachan.'

'If that's all right.'

'Fine as long as you don't stay too long—we want him to rest.' Another glance for Jenna's clothes. 'I think I'd better go in first and explain. Otherwise he'll think you've been in the wars too.'

'Good thinking,' Jenna agreed wryly.

William Strachan looked grey and tired, but his kind blue eyes twinkled at sight of Jenna. 'You've been saving another life, I gather,' he began. 'They'll soon be giving you the Freedom of Port Lindsay.'

'I hope not. That sounds too much like a parting gesture and I don't want to leave yet. Dear William—how are you feeling?'

'Fine, lassie, just fine. So who was it this time?'

'The patient? One of the young Greigs from the

holiday camp. Now will you please tell me how you really feel!'

'I'm as well as can be expected, they tell me. Now if only I could see the monitors. . .'

'Yes, where are they?' she asked, looking round.

'At the nurses' station. This is a custom-built unit.'

'Then I'll sneak a look on my way out.'

'And sneak back to tell me, I hope.'

'Oh, no, I won't. Would you in my place?'

'You're as bad as Rob,' he sighed.

'I'd rather you'd said as good as. . .'

He reached for her hand and squeezed it feebly. 'You think he's a good doctor, do you not?'

'I know he is,' Jenna returned quietly.

'And he's a good man, Jenna.'

'I—I'm beginning to know that too,' she answered on a whisper.

'I hope so, my dear. I hope so,' he said earnestly.

Jenna didn't dare to believe he meant what she hoped he meant. To hide her emotion she bent down and kissed him fondly on the cheek. 'How could a son of yours be anything else?' she asked softly. 'Good-night, dear William. I feel easier in my mind now I've seen you.'

'Is that a medical opinion?' he asked whimsically as she straightened up. She eyed him, head on one side.

'Yes—well, three quarters of one anyway. Now I'd better go before I'm chased away, but I'll be back as soon as I can.'

Jenna went back to Casualty. The boy's relatives would need a lift home if—as she feared—he hadn't made it.

'His condition is unchanged and his mother and aunt are staying with him,' said Sister, sounding more subdued than she had earlier.

Jenna thanked her, apologised for her earlier impatience and left. Unchanged was the best she had hoped for. It would be some time before there could be any improvement.

When Jenna got home, she went straight up to her room to get out of her blood-stained clothing. Then she went down to the kitchen to apologise to Mrs Cullen for being so late for supper. To her surprise, it was Rob who was taking dishes out of the oven. 'Don't tell me that Mrs Cullen has given in her notice,' she implored. 'That's all we need.'

He smiled at her across the table. 'Not to worry. My only contribution to this meal was to keep it warm until you came in.'

'You shouldn't have waited; you must be famished.'

'I'm not long in myself; a call to the coastguard station.' He didn't enlarge on that.

'Which I should have taken—I'm on call.'

'It's rather difficult to be in two places at once,' he pointed out.

'I should have phoned,' Jenna realised, too late. 'Only I was so desperate to get that child to hospital, that I—but I'm forgetting. You don't know anything about that, do you?'

'For heaven's sake sit down and relax now you've got the chance,' he advised. 'And I do know. When Meg told me about the call, which sounded horrific, I phoned the camp to see if you needed help and they told me you'd whisked the child off to hospital. That was good thinking, Jenna. Were you in time?'

'God, I hope so! He was still alive when I left, but he's lost so much blood. . .'

'Whatever the outcome, you did everything you could.' He paused. 'Did you see my father?'

'Yes I did,' she answered, brightening up. 'And he

was looking better than I'd dared to hope. The monitor readings were all satisfactory. The systolic pattern is still erratic, but that's only to be expected.' She stopped. 'I don't know why I'm telling you all this. You know it as well as I do.'

'An update and a second informed opinion are always welcome.'

'Yes, I suppose so. . .' She'd been longing for the chance to speak to him alone ever since Shelagh Donaldson's revealing visit. Now it had come, they were talking about everything but themselves. 'Rob, there's something I want to. . .'

'Relax,' he said, 'and eat your supper before it gets cold. Time enough to talk shop over coffee.'

The phone rang several times during the meal, and each time it was somebody calling to enquire about William. After he had answered it a fifth time, Rob hung up with a growl of protest. 'Folk mean well,' he sighed, 'but it gets a bit wearing after a bit. That must be about the twentieth such call today.'

'And each caller believing he's the only one to think of it,' supposed Jenna.

'Spot on. But then you usually are,' he added thoughtfully.

It was an opening and Jenna took it. 'I'm so glad you said that. It's such a relief to be on the same wavelength at last,' she said earnestly.

'It wasn't your fault that we disagreed at first. I was so damned cagey. . .'

He was only looking at the professional side. 'I'm not surprised you were cagey—considering what you had to put up with from my predecessor.' She hesitated, wondering how best to continue. 'But it's not just the work. Somehow, I feel we're now more, well, sympathetic on a personal level as well.'

'We have my father's heart attack to thank for that. You've been a tower of strength today, Jenna.'

He still doesn't see what I'm getting at and it's my own fault, she realised gloomily. I goofed thoroughly that day at the cottage. And again, when he tried to clear the air. 'I'm glad, and you'd better believe I'll do everything I can to help through this difficult time.' Do you think that's better, you nut?

'You're not—' His voice was husky and he cleared his throat. 'You're not regretting coming to Port Lindsay, then?'

'Not at all. In fact I'd go as far as to say it's about the best thing I've ever done.' Now surely. . .

'A good many doctors would consider a job like this as professional suicide.'

'There's more to life than work,' Jenna said softly. Cue to sweep me off my feet, Rob. . .

But he was frowning. 'I hope you're not falling for that lightweight Nick Lawson,' he said tightly.

Did it take a verbal hatchet to get through to him? 'Nick is very good company, but a little of him goes a very long way.' Jenna leaned towards him across the table and spelled it out. 'For such an intelligent man, you can sometimes be very obtuse, Rob Strachan.'

He looked at her as though he couldn't believe his ears. 'You mean. . .what *do* you mean, Jenna?'

By now, poor Jenna was wondering if she'd misread the situation and *she* was the one who was thick! 'I mean that I'm glad I came to Port Lindsay. I like the town, I like my job and most of all, I like my colleagues. Very much indeed, as it happens.' That was as far as she felt able to go without more encouragement.

'That's very good to know,' he said slowly, almost as though it wasn't what he'd been expecting. 'Because we all like you very much indeed.'

Jenna sighed inwardly. She should have realised that Rob Stachan wasn't the sort of man to be won over quite so easily after a snub such as she'd delivered. He was proud—and she was going to have to work at this.

When the phone rang yet again, she got up quickly, glad of the diversion. 'I'm on call, so I'll answer that.' She listened with horror to the message, then clumsily replaced the phone with a hand that trembled.

Rob had risen too and sensing her distress, he croaked hoarsely, 'Not——?'

She shook her head and turned to him with glistening eyes. 'No—not William. The boy. He——' she swallowed '—he died half an hour ago. That was his father. Oh, Rob! I failed—and he *thanked* me!' She put a hand to her mouth to stifle a sob, just as he caught her and held her close, rocking her gently, stroking her hair and murmuring comfort.

'You didn't fail, little one. You went the minute you got the call. Nobody could have done more.'

'I'm s-sorry—giving way like this. So wimpish. . .'

'Nonsense! You care, and when a doctor stops caring it's time to pack it in.'

'You're such a comfort. Such a comfort. . .'

'It makes a change from being a fault-finding tyrant.'

'I didn't think that—not really.'

'You seemed to—at the time.'

'Such a long time ago, it seems now. Oh, Rob——'

He kissed her. 'And all in the past,' he was whispering when the phone went yet again. He reached for it without freeing Jenna. When she heard him say not to worry, he'd be there directly, she said, 'But I'm on call tonight.'

'And this is one call you'll not be taking,' he said firmly. 'One of my patients whom I've been monitoring closely through a difficult pregnancy has just gone into labour and her mother doesn't think she'll make it to hospital.'

'One life ended and another beginning,' whispered Jenna when he had gone.

CHAPTER SIX

JENNA put more logs on the fire, glancing at the clock as she straightened up. It was more than twenty-four hours since she and Rob had been alone together. When he came in tonight, she intended to make sure that they picked up where they'd left off.

Last night, she'd been determined to wait up for him. A call-out of her own had put paid to that idea. Mrs Cullen had hovered at breakfast, listening avidly while Rob told Jenna about the twins — born more than an hour apart — which had kept him out until the early hours.

Phone calls, Meg with a long list of queries and no chance of a word alone before Jenna started surgery and Rob went out on visits. Failing to synchronise their lunch breaks and then Rob away to see his father before Jenna got home. He couldn't be blamed for that, having arranged to meet the cardiologist at two-thirty to discuss William's case.

Next, seeing Rob's special cases as arranged the previous day, and then being called out to a small boy who had 'swallowed poison'. This turned out to be his mother's contraceptive pills, and taking the time to reassure his distraught parents that, no matter how odd he was feeling now, taking all that hormonal stuff wasn't going to turn him into a little girl meant that Rob had returned and started evening surgery by the time Jenna got back. Calls disrupted supper again. Some were merely enquiries for William, but Rob insisted on answering the emergencies because she would be taking the night calls after his dramatic time the night before.

And to think I overheard Mrs Cullen whispering her worries to Meg about talk in the town if she left Rob alone in the house with 'that woman' if she went away for the weekend as planned. Jenna laughed aloud. The way things were going, the old witch hadn't a thing to worry about.

The front door slammed shut and seconds later Rob came into the room. 'We're in for a storm,' he announced.

'So what's new?' asked Jenna, smiling up at him from where she was sitting, curled up on the couch. 'It's been like this more or less ever since I arrived.'

'And you claim to be glad you came,' he twitted her, dropping down into his favourite chair and stretching his long legs towards the blazing fire.

'And it'll take more than a spot of bad weather to make me change my mind,' she insisted.

'Call this a spot?' he asked. 'You're an optimist, Jen.'

She winced involuntarily and Rob noticed. 'You dislike having your name shortened,' he supposed. 'Sorry.'

Jenna had winced because Jake used to call her Jen and he was the last person she wanted to remember.

'Sheer coincidence,' she claimed. 'I've got a bit of a headache, that's all.'

'I'm not surprised after two such days as you've had. You should have gone to your bed straight after supper.' He then reached out, switched on another lamp and picked up a newspaper.

This was not at all how Jenna had envisaged things when she had built up the fire and turned down the lights. 'You've been having a fairly hectic time yourself,' she countered. 'Aren't you tired too?' Brilliant, Jenna. Now he'll say yes and you'll both retire to your separate rooms!

'A bit, but fortunately I'm finished now. At least——' He looked across at her his expression concerned. 'Is your headache severe, Jenna? If so, I'll take the night calls.'

Jenna wished she'd never invented that blasted headache. 'No, it isn't and no, you will not,' she said more sharply than she'd intended. 'I'm perfectly capable of doing my share.'

'I know that,' he answered quietly, 'but if you're not feeling well——'

'I feel perfectly well. Please don't fuss, Rob! I bet if I were a man——' Jenna stopped, aghast. They could be quarrelling again any minute and she'd thought that was all behind them.

Rob frowned heavily. 'Don't start all that again,' he rapped out.

You've brought this on yourself, Jenna. . . 'I'm sorry I said that,' she said quickly. 'I know you offered out of sheer kindness, but I'm quite fit for work. Honestly. I'm sorry,' she repeated, sitting up and leaning forward earnestly.

He couldn't help being touched by her obvious anxiety. 'It's all right,' he said gently. 'But I think we're both a touch too tired for much constructive conversation tonight. Go to bed, Jenna. I'll be going up myself soon,' he added when she stood up, too dispirited to argue.

She dropped a little curtsy and said, 'Yes, Doctor, anything you say, Doctor,' getting a brief chuckle for her trouble. Quarrel averted, but a long way from the warmth and understanding of the night before. And light years away from those moments in the cottage on the hill.

Rob was unusually late for breakfast next morning, so it wasn't until lunchtime that Jenna discovered why her night's sleep had been undisturbed.

Rob wasn't in yet and Mrs Cullen was upset. 'Straight out on his rounds after surgery, and without so much as a cup of coffee! And after two broken nights too. He'll end up in the hospital with his father, and then where will we all be?'

'What do you mean by *two* broken nights?' demanded Jenna sharply. 'I was on call last night.'

'Were you, now? Well, let me tell you it was Dr Rob who went out about three this morning. Mebbe you forgot to switch the phone through to your room,' she suggested.

'I did no such thing, Mrs Cullen! He must have switched it back!' But it wasn't Mrs Cullen Jenna was mad with. 'I'll sort this out the minute he comes in,' she breathed, getting up from the table and going to the hall, where she'd be sure to catch him, whichever way he came.

He came in via the surgery and dining-room, and Jenna planted herself firmly in his path. 'And what do you think you're playing at?' she demanded fiercely.

Rob blinked, staring down at her blankly. It was well done, but not quite well enough. 'Don't bother playing the innocent—you know quite well why I'm angry! What do you mean by it?'

'If you're steamed up about last night——'

'You switched the phone through to your room, didn't you? How dare you! If you don't trust me, then say so!'

'It had nothing to do with trust, Jenna,' he returned

with dangerous quiet, 'and everything to do with concern. You had a headache. You were also nearly dropping with fatigue. In my opinion, you needed a good night's rest.'

'Your opinion! Tell me, would you have hijacked my night duty if I were a man?'

'You're doing extra work and you'd had a very stressful experience the day before. That took a lot out of you, so—'

'You're dodging the question!' she accused hotly.

'All right then—no, I'd probably not have.'

'Because men can take stressful experiences in their stride and don't go to pieces when they lose a patient?' she asked bitterly.

'We've been down this road before,' he said wearily. 'It's got nothing to do with your being a woman. At least—'

'Surprise me, then! What has it to do with?'

'It was because I care about you, you stupid bitch!' he yelled. 'Though God knows why. I must be out of my mind!' And with that, he pushed roughly past her and stormed into the kitchen.

As a declaration of love it was somewhat less than perfect, but it took all the steam out of Jenna, leaving her weak and weepy. It was, she felt, quite the most beautiful thing anybody had even said to her, and if Mrs Cullen hadn't been in that damned kitchen Jenna would have rushed after Rob and hurled herself into his arms. As it was, she went to the cloakroom to mop up her silly tears and practise a less soppy expression, before going back to her lunch.

Her soup was now cold and by not offering to replace it Mrs Cullen showed clearly where her sympathies lay. Jenna couldn't care less. If Rob loved her, what else mattered?

'I hope you're taking the afternoon off,' Mrs Cullen was cooing to him. 'It *is* your half-day after all—and you could do with a nice lie-down.'

'I have two more house calls to make and then I'm going to see my father,' he stated.

Jenna cleared her throat. Even so, she asked Rob to give William her love in a half-strangled voice.

Rob eyed her sadly. 'I'll do that.'

'And take him those——' She pointed to a basket of fruit and a paperback, lying on the dresser. 'I got them this morning. It only took a minute. . .'

He glanced at the spine of the book. 'William McIllvaney—one of his favourite authors. That was thoughtful of you.'

'I'm not just a—a loudmouth,' she whispered so that the housekeeper wouldn't hear.

He put up a warning hand. 'Do you have much to do this afternoon?' he asked aloud.

'Three more visits and a patient coming whom I saw in surgery yesterday. I'm almost sure Mrs Bunker has SLE, but I'm going over her thoroughly, so as to be sure of my facts before referring her to Rheumatology.'

'Good thinking,' said Rob, getting up from the table. 'No coffee for me, thank you, Jeannie. I'm anxious to get started again.'

'So am I,' said Jenna, also leaping up and with such haste that she banged her knee against the table leg. Ignoring the stinging pain, she hurtled after Rob.

She found him in the tiny dispensary, restocking his case. 'Oh, Rob——'

'Forget it,' he said tersely.

'How can I? You said——'

'Too much.'

'Are you saying you didn't mean it?' She didn't want to believe that.

'Does it matter?' he asked harshly.

Jenna crept close. 'It does to me,' she said softly, laying a hand on his sleeve.

He held out a moment longer before abandoning pretence and putting his arms round her. 'You're a witch,' he said unsteadily, resting his cheek against her hair.

'And witch rhymes with. . .'

His arms tightened their hold. 'That's what I wanted you to forget.'

Just so long as it wasn't the caring bit! 'Actually, I think I liked it better when you called me a pixie,' she whispered.

'I was in a particularly silly mood that day.'

'I rather like you when you're in a silly mood, Rob. . .'

'What's happened to the girl who wasn't looking for *that* sort of relationship?'

'She's—taking stock.'

'And will that take long?'

'That depends,' said Jenna slowly.

'On what?'

'On how much help she gets.'

'Try this for starters,' said Rob, tilting her face up to his and kissing her with a thoroughness and fervour that left her breathless.

'Good heavens,' she murmured when she could.

'Now I'm confused,' claimed Rob. 'Was that meant for approval or horror?'

'We. . .ell,' Jenna was beginning when they heard the street door open and Meg humming tunelessly as she often did.

Rob groaned. 'To be continued in our next,' he said with a sigh as he let Jenna go. He glanced in the mirror, then took out his handkerchief and scrubbed his mouth to get rid of the lipstick.

'Very prudent,' laughed Jenna, watching that. 'You've been caught out before.'

'Who hasn't?' he wondered. 'Lipstick's filthy stuff.'

'It tastes nice, though,' Jenna was saying when Meg came in.

'What does?' Meg asked curiously.

'Ugli fruit—despite its name,' returned Rob, leaving Jenna gasping at his presence of mind.

Meg looked scornful. 'Well, I s'pose it must do, or nobody'd ever buy it, would they?' she asked. 'Now, then, who's doing what this afternoon? I've lost count with all the confusion.'

Rob explained, winked at Jenna over Meg's head and said the sooner he got started, the sooner he'd get home. 'Am I to be allowed to take the on-call tonight, Rob?' Jenna called after him.

He came back as far as the door. 'I think so. Two nights off and one on sounds about right to me,' he added, daring her to contradict him.

'Yes, Doctor, but for whom?' asked Jenna but he didn't come back again.

Her afternoon patient was coming at three and Jenna hoped to fit in her remaining house calls beforehand. Mrs MacKenzie-Smith was first; almost the first patient seen with William on her first day. The time she'd spent in a nursing home since then had left her very dissatisfied with her lonely existence. When Jenna asked why she'd been sent for, the old lady said, 'I want you to find me a good residential hotel, Doctor.'

'Surely you didn't request a house call just for that?' exclaimed Jenna. 'Is your chest being troublesome again? Or perhaps you had a fall——'

'At present, I am perfectly well, thank you, Doctor,

but who's to say what I may have caught, sitting in that stuffy crowded waiting-room?'

The cheek of the woman! Jenna briefly outlined a GP's duties, which certainly didn't include arranging accommodation for purely social reasons. She suggested the tourist board, the social work department and the citizens' advice bureau, then she left.

Next on her list was an ancient, senile and very disturbed old soul, and the distraught granddaughter, struggling to look after her. 'But why you?' wondered Jenna. 'Can't your parents help?'

'Ma dad says she's made his life a misery since the day he was born and he'll not have her in the house. Besides, they've got my mum's dad—not that he's any trouble—but it does mean they've not got the room. And they don't keep too well themselves. Oh, Doctor!' she cried, 'I'm nearly desperate. When ma man's home for his fortnight—he's on the oil-rigs—we row all the time. She keeps coming into our room, so we can't—you know. And she goes anywhere but in the lavvy! Sometimes I feel like taking all the poison I can lay ma hands on and ending it all!'

'Can't you lock your bedroom door?' suggested Jenna, taking what seemed the most straightforward problem first.

'We tried that but she created something awful, throwing things and shouting till the neighbours sent for the polis.'

And shutting psychiatric hospitals was supposed to be progress, thought Jenna, her heart wrung with pity for this poor young woman who was hardly older than herself. 'I'm not promising anything,' she said, 'but I'm going to make a thorough nuisance of myself to try and get your grandmother in somewhere for respite care and assessment.'

The girl was tearfully grateful, but Jenna was worried. If there was anything to be done, then Rob or his father would have done it.

It was almost a relief to go on the third visit, find a patient with a severe bout of gastro-enteritis and practise some straightforward medicine for a change.

Back to the surgery for half an hour with Mrs Bunker and her suspected systemic lupus erythematosus—SLE. There was little doubt. She had the fever, the fleeting joint pains, the skin eruptions, tiredness, weight loss and loss of appetite. And she was in the right age group. Jenna prescribed some palliative treatment, then wrote a persuasive letter to the consultant rheumatologist at the district hospital.

Then she sat back and took stock of her day. Her conclusions were not cheerful. You could do so much for your patients in hospital, just because they were lucky enough to have got in. It was a different thing in general practice. If your patient didn't have one of the life-threatening, dramatic problems currently in vogue—the sort that got into the papers and whipped up so much sympathy—then it was often a bleak prospect. That chronically depressed young girl with the senile grandmother. Her life was disintegrating and she'd soon be a casualty herself. And what about that nice woman she'd seen yesterday who was finding it difficult to run her shop and care for an invalid husband? If only she could get a replacement hip soon, she'd be able to cope. It's a funny old world, Jenna concluded as she picked up the phone, dialled the district hospital and demanded to speak to a psychiatrist. She got one too—a miracle.

'You've got a patient for me, Doctor?' he asked smoothly.

'I've got two,' she said. 'A violent senile old woman

who throws things and a depressed young woman who is dangerously suicidal. As they're both in the same house—alone—I feel justified in bringing them to your notice.'

'That wouldn't be Mrs Perry and her granddaughter, would it?'

Jenna said yes.

'Funnily enough, I've just been looking at a letter from a Dr Strachan about them. They should be getting an appointment quite soon now.'

'How soon is soon?' wondered Jenna.

'Oh, not more than six weeks—say eight to be on the safe side.'

'In that case, you may as well cross them off,' said Jenna, 'because by then, they'll both be dead! The young one by her own hand and the old one from starvation and neglect, since there's nobody else to look after her. End of problem—as I was only saying to an assistant chief constable when he rang up to complain about the constant complaints from neighbours about the old woman's frightening behaviour.' Sometimes, it was necessary to tell a few lies in order to get attention.

'Leave it with me,' he said, sounding less smooth now.

'I will,' said Jenna, 'but not for more than a week.' She rang off before he could ask for the name of her imaginary policeman.

Mrs Cullen was nowhere to be seen and hadn't bothered to set a tea-tray when both her men were absent. Jenna made tea in a mug and ate a couple of stale cream crackers before tackling evening surgery, which was busier than usual.

'That's a compliment to you, Doctor,' said the

retired nurse who occasionally stood in for Meg. 'It shows they've decided that you're all right.'

'I must try to be grateful, then,' returned Jenna with a tired smile, as she stood up and circled her arms in an effort to relieve the tension in her shoulder muscles.

In the kitchen, she found that Mrs Cullen had come and gone again, leaving a Bird's Eye packet and a note on the kitchen table. Rob was there, frowning over the note.

'Is anything wrong?' asked Jenna.

Silently he passed her the note. 'Fish pie just needs heating,' it said. 'I quite like fish pie,' said Jenna.

'So do I,' he said, 'but that's not the point. She's not paid nearly double the going rate to swan off and leave you to fend for yourself after a twelve-hour day and the chance of being called out any minute.'

'You too, Rob.'

'Not so. She knows that with Thursday being my half-day I usually go out for dinner. She was gambling on my doing that today.'

'I'm afraid that Mrs Cullen doesn't like me much,' Jenna admitted ruefully. 'And I've tried so hard not to be a trouble.'

'She doesn't approve of women doctors,' Rob revealed.

'I *knew* there was somebody in this house who didn't,' returned Jenna, and they both laughed.

'Well, that for her and her fish pie,' said Rob, slamming it in the fridge. 'It's scarcely big enough for one, let alone two. We're going to the Lobster Pot.'

'And what will the good folk of Port Lindsay think if they see us eating out together?'

'If anybody so much as glances our way, I'll tell them that Jeannie Cullen has fallen down on the job. She'll be so mortified when she hears that, she'll never try this on again.'

Jenna had been thinking more of speculation about their two selves, but if it didn't bother Rob, it certainly didn't bother her. All the same, she felt she had to warn him against being too hard on the housekeeper. 'You'd never find a better, Rob. She's devoted to you and William.'

'So she should be. As well as being very well paid, she's got her own flat and only has the catering to do—and provided we're adequately fed she can come and go as she likes.' He glanced over Jenna, neat in navy blue skirt and sweater. 'You're looking very nice but I suppose you're wanting to change before we go out.'

'Dressing up would be simply asking for a call,' said Jenna from bitter experience.

'That's true,' Rob agreed and after leaving the restaurant's number on the answering machine, they set off in Jenna's car—just in case.

On the way, he described William's encouraging progress. 'In another week, we could have him home,' he said.

'And then we'll have to handcuff him,' forecast Jenna.

'It didn't take you long to get his measure,' said Rob, laughing.

'I like to think I'm good at reading character,' she returned confidently. Though she'd made a disaster of reading Jake's. . .

'So what do you make of me, then?' asked Rob as they left the car outside the restaurant which was all of three hundred yards from the house.

'Hm! You're rather more complex than your father. Besides——'

'I'm listening,' Rob said softly.

'There's the attraction thing. That always kind of clouds one's judgement.'

His face darkened on the instant. 'Doesn't it just!' he agreed harshly, giving Jenna quite a jolt. Who was he thinking of? Her? Susan? Or another woman altogether?

'Still it does work out all right sometimes,' she urged. 'Not everybody is miserable.'

'On which cheerful note, the couple entered the restaurant hand in hand,' said Rob satirically, reaching towards her.

'Not if they're sensible, they don't—not in Port Lindsay,' she warned with a forced little laugh.

'At least she's well-endowed with common sense,' he muttered, close on her heels. Good grief! Was he compiling a list of pros and cons, then? Yet perhaps that wasn't such a bad idea. She'd had enough of giving way to blind inclination. Could be he had too.

They were given the table in the alcove where Jenna had seen Rob dining with Susan, her sister and her brother-in-law. 'Nice view of the harbour,' she commented, having squeezed out that recollection.

'Then your eyes are better than mine,' said Rob, nodding towards the window, now awash with rain.

'Does it ever overflow?' asked Jenna. 'The harbour, that is.'

'Combine a high spring tide with an easterly gale and Harbour House gets its front steps washed,' said Rob, handing her a menu. 'The monkfish is very good.'

'I know. I had it when I came here the first time.'

'With Nick.' Rob fiddled with the cutlery before asking, 'Are you still seeing him?'

Jenna laughed. 'Don't be daft! What time do I have for seeing anybody these days? And I'm not complaining, just stating a fact.' She laid the menu aside. 'I'll have whatever you're having. After all, I would if we'd stayed at home.'

'Logical too,' he murmured, presumably for the inventory he seemed to be compiling. 'Sometimes, anyway,' he added.

'And what is that supposed to mean?' enquired Jenna with mock severity.

'Whoever heard of a woman who was entirely logical?' he countered provocatively.

They bantered on like that, laughing quite a lot, until the first course came. Jenna eyed it suspiciously. 'What is it?'

'Cullen skink,' said Rob, picking up his spoon and getting to work.

'And what's that, for heaven's sake?'

'Fish soup made with finnan haddies.'

'That's all right then. For a moment, I thought I was about to dine off one of Jeannie's relations.'

His laughter rang round the low raftered room. 'Jenna, you're such a tonic.'

'When I'm in the right company,' she said. She was feeling so happy now, so good with him. Oh, God, please don't let this go wrong, she found herself praying. Yet why should it? They were mature adults and free agents—not starry-eyed impractical children. Jenna looked at him, at the untidy thatch of brown hair, the strong dependable jaw, the intelligent, honest blue eyes and knew beyond all doubt that she had fallen in love with him.

No calls came to spoil the evening and they lingered there, laughing and talking until closing time.

A single light in Mrs Cullen's sitting-room window on the second floor, told that she was in and still up. 'On the alert to make sure we each go to our own room,' whispered Rob as he opened the door.

'What would we do without her?' asked Jenna. Yet she was glad they weren't alone in the house. It was all too easy to let heart and body rule head—and land you in big trouble.

'She's going away for the weekend, though,' whispered Rob as they crept up the stairs.

'No, she isn't. I overheard her telling Meg. She's decided to stay and play chaperon.'

'Blast,' said Rob, but he didn't sound too annoyed. Outside Jenna's door, he put his arms loosely round her shoulders. 'Extra thinking time for you,' he said softly. 'Use it wisely, my dear little pixie. You're having the most deplorable effect on me. . .' His arms slid round her pliant body, pulling her near. Then he kissed her, suspending thought and leaving her only with feelings that clamoured urgently for expression.

A light was switched on on the upper landing and the housekeeper called down, 'Is that you, Dr Fielding? There was a call about twenty minutes ago. It sounded urgent.'

Unwillingly, Jenna extricated herself from Rob's arms. 'Thank you, Mrs Cullen,' she called back. 'I'm going as soon as I've collected my case.' Then she whispered guiltily to Rob, 'How awful! We forgot to check.'

Rob was frowning up the stairs towards the housekeeper's flat. 'Not so fast. How did she know there'd been a call—unless she went down and switched on the answering machine? And why didn't the caller ring the Lobster Pot?'

'Just what I'm about to find out,' said Jenna. She reached up and kissed him on the lips. 'Goodnight, dear Rob. I'll see you in the morning.' Then she hurried downstairs.

As Rob had suspected, there was no message on the

answering machine, so Mrs Cullen's sole object had been to break up the imagined scene on the landing. Jenna was suddenly very angry. Whatever her relationship with Rob, the housekeeper had no right to interfere. If he found out what she was doing, then her happy, well-rewarded days at Harbour House were numbered.

The phone rang just as Jenna was about to switch it through to her room. 'Oh, Doctor, can ye come? It's Matt,' said the caller. 'He's been awful sick and now he's burning up and going drowsy—'

Jenna seized a pencil. 'Name and address, please.' A woman's work was never done. Especially if she was a doctor.

On Saturday morning, Rob took surgery while Jenna did house calls. After lunch, he would visit William while she sat by the phone. Rob had offered to let Jenna visit, but she insisted that he was the one his father would want to see. They were hoping that the good citizens of Port Lindsay would manage to keep sickness at bay and allow them a quiet evening together by the fire.

Her calls took longer than expected and Jenna dashed into the kitchen, expecting to find that Rob had already had his meal. The table was set, but only Mrs Cullen was there.

'Surely Rob's not still in surgery!' exclaimed Jenna.

'No. Surgery finished some time ago, I believe.'

'He's waiting lunch for me, then,' supposed Jenna.

'That was his intention until the visitor arrived. You're to join them in the sitting-room.'

'A visitor—how exciting. Who is it?'

'I wasn't introduced,' said Mrs Cullen, smirking still. But her eyes were cold.

Jenna didn't understand the smirk but the attitude was consistent—especially as Rob had read the riot act about Thursday's supper, or lack of it. She stopped by the hall mirror just long enough to tidy her hair, before opening the sitting-room door. She halted, dumbstruck, three paces inside the room, ashen white and ready to faint. The perfectly tailored Viking type lounging at ease on the hearthrug was Jake. Her anxious eyes turned to Rob, standing rigid by the window, feet astride and arms folded across his old tweed jacket. His expression was brooding and fierce.

Next moment, he was blocked from sight when Jake bounded across to her. 'Jenna, my darling. So wonderful to see you——'

She was so shocked that he actually managed to get his arms round her before she came to. 'Damn you, let me go!' she hissed. 'Rob——' But Rob had gone, slamming the door behind him.

Now Jenna was consumed with rage. She contrived a sharp kick to Jake's shin, leaving a dirty mark on his beautiful pale grey trousers. 'You bloody hypocrite!' she blazed. 'What the hell do you mean by this?'

'Darling—such language. This isn't like you.'

'Nothing about the me I am now is anything like the naïve little mouse you knew! You've wasted your time, coming here.'

'We belong together, Jenna. You know that,' he purred with an assurance that was almost frightening in its certainty. 'I've come to take you home.'

Somehow she had got to make him understand that his hold on her was broken for ever. 'Then you'll have to knock me out and kidnap me,' she said scathingly, 'because I'll never go willingly. I told you we were finished before I left and I'm telling you again now.'

'Deep down, we still love each other, Jenna.'

His confidence was infuriating. 'Love never came into our relationship! You don't know the meaning of the word and I was simply besotted, poor fool that I was. But not any more. You tried my patience once too often—and that cured me! You're weak, amoral and totally self-centred. The only wonder is why it took me so long to find out!'

'You're surprised to see me,' he said less confidently. 'I should have let you know I was coming. . .'

'I wish you had—then I'd have been elsewhere!' She fixed him with a look of total loathing. 'Oh, go away, you posturing idiot! You sicken me.'

She had got through to him at last. 'I do believe you're fancying yourself in love with that rustic hulk who opened the door to me,' he sneered. 'But I doubt if he's very enamoured of you after what he's heard from me!'

'Rob will understand when I tell him the truth,' said Jenna, sounding more confident than she felt.

'I wouldn't bank on it, my dear. He's not the type to stomach another man's discarded mistress for a wife.'

He'd always been expert at putting in the knife where it would hurt most. 'God, but you really are the pits,' she breathed. 'You wouldn't know the truth of anything if it jumped up and bit you. You're nothing but mouth and trousers! Now get out before I ring for the police and have you thrown out!' She had already lifted the phone and was looking quite furious enough to do that.

In one last attempt at bluster, Jake said, 'You're making a big mistake, Jenna, if you think I'll take you back after this.'

'I can live with it,' she yelled after him.

His slamming of the front door galvanised her into action. She ran to the kitchen, where the housekeeper was clearing the untouched meal from the table. 'Where's Rob?' she demanded recklessly.

'Dr Rob has gone to see his father,' Mrs Cullen replied repressively. 'And he told me that you would be lunching with your gentleman friend.'

'That man is no friend of mine!' Jenna denied fiercely.

'Really? I got quite the opposite impression.'

'Then your intuition is sadly at fault,' said Jenna. 'And now, if you please, I would like some food on a tray. I'll have lunch in my room while I write some reports.'

They stared at one another for several long seconds; a battle of wills which Jenna won.

She carried the unwanted tray upstairs and left it on the table while she paced up and down, up and down, trying to decide how best to explain things to Rob. But all the time, uppermost in her mind, was Jake's spiteful remark about Rob not being the kind of man to want another man's discarded mistress. She was horribly afraid that Jake was right.

CHAPTER SEVEN

JENNA was out on a call when Rob came home and when she got back he had gone out again. When she switched the answering machine to listen for any more calls, she found that he had substituted her tape for one of his own. 'This is Dr Rob Strachan,' she heard. 'In emergency, please phone Port Lindsay 41292. Thank you.' Brief and to the point, as ever. They hadn't decided who was to be on tonight. Now he had taken things out of her hands. Of course, she could regain control by switching the phone through to her room, but that would only infuriate him further.

She wondered where he was. With Susan perhaps? She opened the telephone directory and sure enough the number on the tape was the number of the MacArthur farm. Jenna was pierced by a shaft of bitter jealousy. It hadn't taken long for him to go back to her—if he'd ever really broken it off. Her sister would be overjoyed.

Wearily, Jenna plodded up to her room. This was going to make it harder than ever to explain about Jake. It was obvious from the way he was avoiding her that Rob didn't want to hear her side of it. Damn you, Jake! You were always so convincing. But whether Rob believed her or not, she would *make* him listen. She owed it to herself.

Jenna switched on the television, switched off again and tried to read. Supper time came and went without a summons. So what? She was too miserable to eat anyway. At half-past eight, somebody knocked on her door. She flew to open it, her heart pounding madly.

Mrs Cullen stood there with a tray. 'I'm sorry to be late with your supper, Doctor,' she said stiffly, 'but I didn't realise you were still here until I came home and noticed the light in your room.'

Jenna was too dazed to do more than take the tray with muttered thanks and shut the door. Still here, she'd said. Did she hope that Jenna had gone off with the 'visitor'? Jenna sat down and took the cloth off the tray. Soup, Thursday's rejected fish pie—with some steamed broccoli—biscuits and cheese. Mrs Cullen hadn't exactly over-reached herself, but she had complied with the rules as spelt out by Rob.

When midnight had come and gone and Rob hadn't returned, Jenna undressed and got into bed. One o'clock, two. . . Did he mean to stay out all night? And then she heard his step on the stairs and his bedroom door open and shut. She got up, put on her dressing-gown, crossed the landing and tapped gently on his door.

So far he'd only removed his jacket. When he opened the door, he stared. 'You!' and then, 'Do you know what time it is?'

'Yes,' she said, 'but we have to talk.'

'If you'd said that a week ago, there might have been some point,' he said acutely. 'Now it's too late—in more ways than one.'

When he made to shut the door, Jenna slipped into the room. 'You've been deliberately avoiding me all day and will probably do the same tomorrow. You've got to listen to me, Rob. You owe me that much.'

'All right,' he said, 'but make it brief. It's been a hell of a day.'

'I've not exactly enjoyed it either,' she said quietly.

Then, leaning against his wardrobe for support, she said through stiff lips, 'About Jake. I don't know what he told you, but I imagine he was very persuasive—painting me all black and himself whiter than snow. The terrible thing is, he probably believes it!' She paused, her breath catching in her throat. 'I met him in my first job. He was the registrar. He was so kind and helpful and I thought he was wonderful. When the nurses sniggered and Sister warned me so tactfully, I thought they were all jealous. To me, he was just too good to be true—and I was right about that at least, though I didn't realise it until we'd been living together for about a year. By then, we were working in different hospitals. That was his idea. He said that working together could stale our relationship. What he meant was it would cramp his style. The first time, I believed him when he told me that the girl who'd come crying to me to let him go had made all the running. I thought he was God's gift, so why wouldn't others? I forgave him the next time too—and the next. I'd invested so much effort and emotion in that relationship that I couldn't face up to his lack of commitment. Especially when he kept insisting that he couldn't bear to lose me.

'He said he went to Edinburgh to further his career, and I believed that too. Now I wonder if Leeds was getting too hot to hold him. Less than a year later, he was at it again. Then something inside me snapped. He was never going to change and I'd had enough. I resolved to get as far away from him as I could. That's why I applied to come here.'

Rob had listened intently, not stirring. He was still silent and motionless. She'd told him as honestly as she could and it hadn't been enough. With a heavy sigh, Jenna said, 'As God's my witness that was the truth,

Rob, whether you believe me or not.' Then she slipped quickly out of the room and ran back to her own.

He was only seconds after her. He shut her bedroom door and leaned against it. 'I do believe you,' he said jerkily. 'Apart from anything else, I took an instant dislike to that man. But why didn't you tell me when you realised how things were—were developing between us?'

'Pride, Rob. It's a terrible thing is pride. I didn't want you to know how weak and gullible I could be.'

'Do you imagine that I've never made a mistake?' he asked harshly. 'Has nobody here told you about Isobel?'

'I've met nobody but patients and the people in this house since I came. And Nick, of course,' she remembered.

'And he may not know about her.' In the dim light shed by the bedside lamp, his blue eyes were dark pools of pain and sadness. 'We married as soon as we qualified and when I tell you that she is the female counterpart of that Jake creature, you'll realise why it ended in divorce three years later.'

As soon as we qualified, he'd said, so if Isobel was a doctor that explained a lot. Like why Mrs Cullen disliked female doctors and why Rob hadn't welcomed her—especially after her predatory predecessor. 'We've neither of us been lucky in love, have we?' she asked in a small voice.

'Or very wise. *Now* do you understand?'

'I hope we're both seeing a lot more clearly now,' Jenna said softly going up to him, hopeful and appealing. 'Oh, Rob——'

'Jenna.' She was in his arms, straining close, yearning to comfort and heal and be comforted and healed in her turn.

'My darling,' she murmured against his demanding mouth. 'It's all right. Everything—is all right. . .' She could feel him hardening and was rejoicing in their mutual need when the sound—faint but unmistakable—of the phone ringing in his room, penetrated their fevered consciousness.

He groaned and his arms tightened momentarily around her before he forced himself to let her go. 'Of all the abysmal timing,' he muttered.

'I know, darling, I know. Better now, though, than later. . .'

'Dr Rob. Dr Rob,' called a voice from above.

'Does that bloody woman never sleep?' he wondered, wrenching the door open. 'Jenna——'

'I'm not going anywhere,' she said softly.

She lay awake, eager for his return. He was gone some time, and when he did come back, he went straight to his room.

Mrs Cullen was on guard in the kitchen when Jenna went down to breakfast; fussing over Rob, pouring his coffee and plying him with toast.

'Oh, dear, am I very late?' asked Jenna.

'Yes,' said the housekeeper.

'No,' said Rob firmly. 'It's Sunday, so why hurry? There's no surgery.'

'Thank you.' Jenna risked a small smile for him.

Having his back to Jeannie, Rob was able to wink back. It wasn't much, but it was some comfort. She'd lain awake for ages after he came in, wondering why he didn't come back to her. And imagining all sorts of reasons. Mostly unflattering.

Mrs Cullen brought Jenna her porridge. 'I trust your dinner was satisfactory last night, Doctor,' she said for Rob's benefit.

'I only wanted something light, so it fitted the bill nicely, thank you,' Jenna answered.

Mrs Cullen eyed her narrowly, suspecting sarcasm, and she was right in that. 'Who's on duty today?' she asked next.

They hadn't decided. 'I think I should take the calls today,' said Jenna to Rob. 'After all, you had a disturbed night.'

'How do you know that?' demanded the housekeeper rashly.

Rob glared at her, making her flush. 'There are very few nights without at least one call, so that was a reasonable assumption on Dr Fielding's part. Was it not?' he insisted, getting a reluctant nod of agreement. 'Besides, if she was awake at the time, she probably heard the phone.'

'I did, as it happens,' supported Jenna.

'About today,' said Rob. 'If you'll take the morning, I'll do the afternoon. Then you can visit my father—I know he'd like to see you. I'd do the whole day, but there's a great pile of paperwork that's crying out for attention.'

'Sounds fair enough to me,' said Jenna, brightening up. Because if Rob was going through to the surgery, they'd have a chance to talk. Surgery was outside the province of their self-appointed guardian of morals.

The first call came in before Jenna had finished her breakfast. 'No hurry, Doctor, but Mammy says if you could call in some time and take a look at ma Dad, she'd be awful grateful. He's kinda drowsy and not making much sense.'

Looking up the records and finding that Mr Mathieson of Dromore Road was a diabetic, Jenna dashed off at once.

Having completed his emergency treatment, Jenna

asked if he'd had any more episodes like this. 'He used to, Doctor, until Dr Rob gave him a richt guid telling for not watching the beer. He's been a lot better since.' Mrs Mathieson scratched the side of her nose. 'Only last night, one of his mates off the boat had a bit of a ceilidh on account of having won the pools. And Dougal got carried away. Had one too many, I'm thinking.'

More than one, thought Jenna privately. 'Beer's the worst thing for a diabetic because of its high sugar content,' she said. 'It's very hard to have to keep saying no, but it's that—or harmful episodes like today. I think I'll ask Dr Rob to look him over as he's familiar with his case.'

'Thank you, Doctor. If anybody can put the fear o' God into him, it's Dr Rob.' Quite a tribute, that, in such a God-fearing community as a fishing port.

When Jenna got home again, Mrs Cullen was making coffee. 'There's nothing quite like the smell of freshly brewed coffee,' observed Jenna, trying to be friendly.

'That's for Dr Rob,' said Mrs Cullen.

Well, it would be, wouldn't it? 'I'll take it to him. I have to go to the surgery anyway.'

'He's not in the surgery—he's in the house,' said Mrs Cullen with a triumphant smirk. 'And there's been another call. You're to ring this number right away.'

She had to relay the message, but did she have to do it so bossily? Jenna controlled her impatience and said silkily, 'No wonder Harbour House runs so smoothly with you at the helm.'

This time it wasn't a call out; just an anxious daughter with a query about correct dosage. 'Mother's so vague, Doctor, and I don't understand the directions on the label.'

'Read it to me,' Jenna invited. 'What it boils down

to,' she said afterwards, 'is two tablets three times daily after meals. It's only a mild antacid, so if she's made the odd mistake, there's no harm done.' I must have a word with that locum pharmacist, decided Jenna as she replaced the phone, ask him to be a bit more basic in his instructions. Not everybody understands how many milligrams of this and that are contained in each pill.

'That didn't take long,' observed Mrs Cullen suspiciously when Jenna returned so soon. Was she suggesting that Jenna was being neglectful?

'As with your work, some of my jobs take less time than others,' retorted Jenna. 'I hope it's safe to assume that we *both* know what we're doing.' She left the housekeeper seething and went looking for Rob. She found him in the rarely used study. The desk was littered with papers and he was frowning. When he saw her face, he accused Jenna of frowning.

'I hope it's not me you're mad at,' he said.

'That woman. . .!' She told him about her recent exchange with Jeannie.

'She's certainly overstepping the mark these days,' he agreed, 'but it sounds to me as if you got the best of that round.'

'Yes, I think I did, but it shouldn't be necessary.' The housekeeper and her vagaries were a long way down the list of things Jenna wanted to talk about with Rob. Judging by the state of the room though, this was no time for personal matters. 'Could you use some help?' she asked.

'I thought you'd never ask,' he said gratefully. 'Dad usually does the paperwork. It's this damn forecast of expenses. What the hell do they expect?'

Jenna glanced over it. 'Good question, when we're not fortune-tellers. I can tell you what my uncle in Yorkshire does, though. He refers back to the last half-year's figures and then adds fifteen per cent. It seems to work. Alternatively, I could ask William what he does when I see him later.'

'I'd rather spare him if I can. Tell me some more about your uncle's creative accounting, Jenna.'

They worked until lunchtime and it was nice; harmonious, cosy and profitable. Little remained to be done when they were called to the kitchen. But Jenna was no nearer knowing why Rob hadn't come back to her room last night. And after lunch she was going to the hospital to see William.

By the time she got home, it was dark. For once the air was still and the sea calm. The harbour lights lay reflected in the still water and danced over the fishing fleet tied up row on row abreast. Even without the tie-up ban, there'd have been no fishing on a Sunday. The fishermen of Port Lindsay were both superstitious and deeply religious.

Rob's car was in its usual place on the cobbled quayside and a chink of light showed between the heavy curtains in the sitting-room. The windows of Mrs Cullen's flat on the second floor were in darkness. Was she out, then? Jenna parked quickly and hurried eagerly into the house.

'Nice timing,' smiled Rob as she joined him. He lifted the teapot questioningly.

'Yes, *please*,' she said. 'They gave me a cup at the hospital when William got his, but it wasn't exactly a choice blend. Oh, Rob! He's looking almost better than I've ever seen him—and they're talking of letting him home mid-week.'

He handed her tea and a buttered scone. 'Just time to run up a strait-jacket, then,' he returned with a rueful grin.

'He'll certainly need watching,' she agreed. 'He was asking me if *I* was feeling the strain, but of course I said no.'

'And are you?' he asked quickly.

'Not on account of the work,' she answered pointedly.

'I had a word with Jeannie while you were out,' he revealed, but it wasn't she Jenna had been referring to. 'I pointed out what a fix we'd be in for the next wee while if anything should happen to upset you and cause you to leave. I think she got the message.'

Jenna didn't like the matter-of-fact way he had mentioned her leaving. 'It would take rather more than her hostility to make me desert,' she said quietly.

'I'd like to think that nothing could,' Rob retorted.

Jenna met his glance and held it. 'There's one thing that could,' she returned steadily.

'Then for heaven's sake tell me what it is!'

'If you wanted me to go, I don't think I'd even wait to pack.'

He looked stunned. 'I don't want you to go—why would I? Have you gone mad?'

Jenna examined her nails, running a thumb along their tips. 'Once or twice today, I've wondered if you were—were having a sort of nasty *déjà vu* about last night. After all, I'm not the first assistant to—to burst into your room in the middle of the night, am I?'

'Jenna! How can you say such a thing?' He got up and came over to her, pulling her to her feet. 'My dearest girl, there's no comparison—none whatever!'

'Are you sure?' she persisted, because Jake's spiteful parting thrust had been gnawing at her all day like an aching tooth.

'Of course I'm sure! That woman didn't attract me

in the least—and you do. You know that! Besides, she had the morals of an alley-cat.'

Jenna shivered. 'Some people might say the same about me. . .'

He held her off, staring down into her eyes in puzzlement. 'I've known from the beginning that you tend to underrate yourself, but this is ridiculous. You, amoral? What nonsense.'

'I just thought—kind of wondered; living with Jake the way I did. . .'

He pulled her close again. 'I thought we had all this out last night. I can't pretend to admire your taste, but you were obviously sincere about the relationship. A less moral woman would have given up on him long before you did.' His face clouded over. 'I didn't put up with half what you did before I broke with Isobel.'

'You were married to her,' she remembered.

'Be thankful you never took that step. Getting divorced is a difficult and painful business. I'd not wish it on anybody.'

'So you don't think. . .that wasn't why you didn't. . .'

'Didn't what?'

'Come back to my room last night,' she whispered.

He kissed her tenderly, lingeringly. 'By the time I got home, I'd had time to cool down and think. This thing has sprung up between us so quickly. How could I be sure you weren't just on the rebound? And you'd obviously been wondering that yourself when you drew back before. You need a breathing space, after all you've been through. This is very important, Jenna. I don't believe either of us is looking for a quick fix. We've got nothing to lose by gaeing canny, as we say up here. There's also a very appropriate old saying about whit's for ye nae goin' by ye.'

That sounded good, but Jake and Isobel had definitely not been for them—and they'd not gone by. The front door opened and closed.

'Who's that?' wondered Jenna.

'That'll be Nanny. She's been out to tea and even though I told her not to hurry back, she obviously doesn't trust me to switch on the oven for the joint.'

'That's her story anyway,' returned Jenna.

'You're shrewd,' said Rob, kissing her lightly. 'Jenna——'

'Yes, Rob?'

'I feel much happier now we've talked. We know where we stand now.'

But do we? she wondered as they drew apart when the housekeeper tapped on the door. They'd talked about the past, but what of the present? He hadn't said a word about Susan MacArthur.

William came home on Wednesday. It being her half-day, Jenna was the one to fetch him. 'I'm so looking forward to getting back to normal,' he said when she'd settled him in the car.

'It depends on what you mean by normal,' said Jenna. 'You're going home and that's lovely for all of us, but you're not going back to work for at least a month.'

'I don't think——' he began, and Jenna repeated what the cardiologist had told them. 'If you weren't coming home to a medical household, you'd still be in hospital. And if you don't behave for me, I know you'll do as Rob tells you,' she added.

'What chance have I got between the two of you?' he wondered with a mock sigh.

'None—and I'm glad you realise it.' She spoke firmly, but she reached out to squeeze his hand. How quickly I've become fond of both these Strachans, she realised. And to think I worried all the way to Port Lindsay because I thought I was making a mistake!

Harmony had reigned at Harbour House these last few days. Work ensured that Jenna and Rob had spent little time together, but the few shared moments had been very sweet: full of laughter and tenderness and a growing awareness of shared interests and views to add to the strong attraction between them. It was all as different as it could be from the anxieties and tensions of her time with Jake.

William's homecoming was positively regal, with people waving and calling out good wishes as they drove through the town. The house was full of flowers and Mrs Cullen had prepared a tea fit for a king. 'If I were to sample even half of that lot, I'd be back in hospital by nightfall,' supposed William, eyeing the trolley.

'You and me both,' said Jenna laughing. 'If not from a cholesterol surge, then a bad attack of indigestion.'

'She means well,' said William, sitting down in his favourite chair and looking round the room with a sigh of contentment.

'I know,' Jenna agreed wryly.

When Rob came in some time later, he handed Jenna a pile of letters and a couple of small parcels. 'These were on the hall table. Did you not see them?'

'No—I was too keen to get William to the fire. The heater in my car isn't working properly.'

'Where is he?' asked Rob. 'Is he OK or have you put him to bed?'

'He's in the kitchen talking to Mrs C, right now.'

Rob relaxed visibly. 'How do you find him?'

'Amazingly well.' She laid aside her mail to be looked at later.

'You're very popular,' he said, watching her. 'Is it your birthday?'

'Not till Saturday, but I'm not that keen on remembering.'

'But you're down to work. We can't have that.'

What can't we have?' asked William, coming back just then.

'Jenna working on her birthday.' Rob looked his father over with a professional eye. 'Yes, I think you'll do, you old warrior, but no stepping out of line.'

'Much chance between the two of you,' grumbled William. 'When is your birthday, Jenna? We must ask Mrs Cullen to bake you a cake.'

She'll love that, thought Jenna wryly, as Rob said Saturday, and he'd decided to ask Dr Porteous to do an evening locum.

Jenna kept repeating that she didn't want a celebration, but she wasn't heeded. Then the practice phone rang and an argument ensued about who should take the call. Jenna was officially off, but had had her tea, while Rob had not. She settled it by running out of the room and leaving the two Strachans together.

Jenna gave herself a final appraisal in her bedroom mirror. Her green eyes, usually so serious, were positively sparkling. It was exciting to be dressed up for an evening out after so long. A gala evening out. At William's suggestion, Rob was taking her to a very upmarket hotel down the coast for her birthday dinner. Not that Rob had needed much urging; just hadn't wanted to leave his father alone so soon after coming out of hospital. But the minister was here for supper and a chat and Dr Porteous, a GP recently retired home to his native town, was looking after the practice.

'Are you not ready yet?' Rob called plaintively from the landing.

'Coming!' Jenna snatched up her coat.

'You look absolutely wonderful,' breathed Rob, his eyes devouring her.

'You don't look so bad yourself,' said Jenna, who had never seen him looking so smart. Such an expensive-looking dark grey suit. He'd tamed his untidy dark hair, too, and hadn't stinted on the aftershave. 'Quite the dandy,' she laughed.

Rob winced. 'Lord, I hope not! That's not me at all.'

Jenna squeezed his arm. 'You're right. There's nothing of the dandy about you. You do look nice, though—and all in my honour.'

'I'd not have gone to all this trouble for anyone else,' he assured her, running a finger round the collar of a split new shirt.

'I find that very encouraging,' said Jenna.

'You do? So may I take it that all this finery you're wearing was just for me?'

'Well, I'm not out to ensnare anyone else,' she told him pertly.

'You'd better be telling the truth about that.' When he helped her into her coat, his hands lingered on her shoulders and before he let her go he kissed the lobe of her ear, causing a tiny *frisson* of pleasure.

'One of your erogenous zones?' he asked on a murmur.

'It's a fairly common one, I'm told,' she returned with scarcely a tremor.

'There's nothing common about you, my girl,' he returned as he took her hand and towed her down the stairs. He opened the sitting-room door to tell William they were leaving and William called back that they were to enjoy themselves and not hurry home.

'An enlightened parent is such a blessing to an impetuous young chap like me,' Rob said absurdly, sending Jenna into peals of laughter.

'And to think I thought you so fierce and unapproachable when I first came,' she confessed.

'And now?' he asked, opening the car door for her.

'Stop fishing,' she ordered.

'But everybody fishes around here,' he protested. 'This is a fishing port.'

'And you're a doctor—not a fisherman.'

'Is that an invitation to examine you?' he asked silkily.

'You're in a wicked mood tonight,' said Jenna. 'I wonder if I was wise to come?'

He got in quickly and drove off at speed. 'Before you change your mind,' he explained as they passed the Lobster Pot.

'This is so exciting,' said Jenna. 'I feel as though I was being made off with.'

'A common feminine fantasy—or so I'm told.'

'Are you saying that I'm dreaming?' she asked. 'Oh, *what* a disappointment! I suppose that any moment now I'll wake up and realise I'm really on my way to a case.'

'You can forget doctoring for tonight—unless the waiter has a fit and drops soup down your neck.'

'If he did, my language would be anything but medical, I assure you. This dress cost me an arm and a leg.' And I've never worn it, because Jake never remembered to take me out, birthday or no birthday.

'And from what I saw of it before you got your coat on, it was worth every penny.'

'Who would have thought that big, fierce Dr Rob Strachan would turn out to be such a pussycat?' marvelled Jenna.

'Or that demure, prim little Dr Jenna Fielding would turn out to be such a siren?'

'Don't stop—I like it,' she said.

'I shall have to in a minute,' chuckled Rob. 'We're nearly there.'

Lindsay Castle Hotel was a surprising place to find in this part of the world. It was tucked away in a small wooded glen through which the Lindsay Water flowed down to the sea. 'The Lindsays once owned half of Angus,' Rob explained. 'Then they fell on evil times and the place was practically a ruin when some distant cousins of theirs rescued it and turned it into a hotel. Now, coming here to fish and play golf is considered to be a very upmarket thing to do.'

'And do you do either of those things, Rob?' asked Jenna. There was still so much she didn't know about him.

'When do I get the time for such frivolities?' he was asking when the car rounded a bend and the floodlit castle came into view.

Jenna was enchanted. 'It's like something out of Disney,' she breathed, taking in the tiny windows, pepperpot turrets and vast studded oak door. 'But it must be the devil to run—especially as a hotel. All those spiral stairs and so many floors.'

'Wait until we park,' said Rob. 'From here, you can only see the original medieval tower.'

Sure enough, when they had driven round the old part, there was a graceful three-storey eighteenth-century addition, with a long terrace and shallow steps up to a pillared entrance. 'How elegant,' said Jenna admiringly.

'Yes. By the time this bit was built, the neighbours came calling in carriages—not with hordes of bearded clansmen hooching and wielding claymores.'

'What *is* a claymore, Rob?'

'The ignorance of you English! A claymore is a great two-handled sword. The highlander's traditional weapon. There's one on show in the Great Hall.'

'The men must have been huge in those days,' reckoned Jenna when she saw it.

'And well-muscled. It was the diet of oatmeal and tatties and salt herring that did it.'

'Not all that tasty-sounding, but obviously more healthy than chips and cream with everything. Do look at those dresses, Rob. They must have cost a fortune.'

'Yes, all four limbs,' he agreed. 'But don't fret, Pixie. None of those mature matrons looks a patch on you. Which is probably why all the men are ogling you and envying me,' he added on a whisper as they crossed the expanses of tartan carpet to the bar.

'We must be about the youngest couple here,' Jenna realised, when they were sipping their dry sherries.

'I hope I haven't made a mistake,' he murmured. 'Perhaps your idea of a birthday treat is a rave-up in a disco.

Jenna giggled. 'I can't remember the last time I went to a disco.' Her face clouded over. Or anywhere very much at all, she realised. Jake hadn't wasted his money taking her further than the Chinese restaurant on the corner, once in a while. But then he'd needed all his spare cash for impressing his latest conquest on those evenings when she'd thought he was busy with his hospital research.

'This is now, not then,' whispered Rob with unerring insight as he put the menu in her hands.

She looked at him gratefully, thrilling to the warmth in his deepset blue eyes. How could she ever have thought them cold? 'This is very embarrassing,' she said after a moment. 'Nothing is priced.'

'They assume that if you need to know the cost you can't afford to be here,' he said carelessly.

'Then you shouldn't have brought me,' she said, conscience-stricken. 'The Lobster Pot would have been fine.'

'Call it payment for all the overtime you've been doing lately. I'm going to have the *boeuf en croute*. What about you?'

'Tay salmon, I think—please.'

'At the risk of sounding corny, your wish is my command, o, pixie.' Rob gave the order and said they'd have avocado to start with, followed by poached turbot, before their main courses.

'Have you won the pools too?' she wondered, laughing.

'I wish I had. Why—has somebody we know?'

She told him about Dougal Mathieson and Rob said what hell it must be to be a diabetic when you wanted to celebrate. 'But that's enough about work. Tell me what you were doing on your last birthday.'

Crying my eyes out because Jake had forgotten it. 'I can't remember,' she said.

'Well, the one before, then?' That year, she'd been packing to follow Jake to Edinburgh, while her friend the ward sister sat on the end of her bed, begging her to have more sense. She should have listened. Still, if she'd not come north, she'd not have met Rob. . . 'I can't remember that either,' she said.

'I wasn't prying,' he said gently. It's just that I know so little about you.'

'You shall have my life history over dinner—if you really want it,' Jenna promised as they followed the restaurant manageress to the dining-room.

'You've not had it easy, little one,' said Rob when she'd told him about her mother's early death and her father's prompt remarriage to a stepmother who believed that the best place for ready-made children was a boarding school at the other end of the country.

'I don't know what I'd have done if my uncle and aunt hadn't retired early from that African mission hospital and gone into practice in the Yorkshire Dales.'

'And inspired you to become a doctor.'

'No, that was something I'd been set on ever since my mother's death. I was only eight and for years after I was convinced that she wouldn't have died if only I'd known what to do. They backed me to the hilt, though.'

'Had they no children of their own, your uncle and aunt?'

'Yes—five. And as they said, with such a brood one more didn't make much difference.'

'Just so.' Rob poured more wine into her glass. 'One of a large family not your own,' he remarked slowly. 'I can see now why you fell prey to that man. He was probably the first person to make you feel special.'

'That's exactly how it was—at first. Oh, Rob, you're so wise!'

'Not really. It had to be something like that. You're no fool, Jenna.'

'I'm not so sure about that, though I hope I've learned some sense now. But that's enough about me. Tell me about yourself, Rob. You're an only child. . .'

'No,' he said. 'I had a sister once.' He told her how she'd died of meningitis a week before her twelfth birthday and of the grief that pervaded Harbour House for so long after that.

Jenna stretched out a hand to cover his which was lying clenched on the fine linen tablecloth. 'Oh, Rob—dear Rob, I'm so sorry. I'd never have asked if I'd dreamed——'

His look was warmly reassuring and intimate. 'We've

both had our dark days, Jenna, but let's hope the worst is now behind us.' He smiled at her across the flowers and candles. 'Are we not a right pair of masochists? This is supposed to be a celebration, not a wake. So no more moping. And that's an order, Doctor!'

He was as good as his word and kept her laughing through the rest of that heavenly meal and the excellent coffee that followed in the pretty drawing-room next door.

As they were leaving, a red-faced man lumbered unsteadily to his feet and barred their way, peering short-sightedly at Rob. 'I thought it was you,' he said triumphantly, 'but that's not the lovely Susan. So what are you playing at, you naughty boy?'

'You're drunk, man!' said Rob angrily, pushing Jenna ahead of him without any introductions.

'Who was that?' she asked inevitably.

'Just a man I know.'

'I'd guessed his sex,' she said. 'I was wondering how he fits in.'

'He doesn't,' he said shortly. 'He's just a friend of a friend.'

'A friend of your friend Susan MacArthur?' She had to know.

He looked down at her warily. 'Of her father's, actually.'

'So by this time tomorrow she will almost certainly know that you were here tonight with a strange woman.'

'She knows already,' Rob said mulishly. 'I told her.'

Well, he would have to tell her something when he usually spent his Saturday evenings with her. 'I do hope she doesn't mind,' said Jenna.

'Of course she doesn't—why should she? We're just good friends. Jenna, what *is* this?'

'Just what I was wondering,' she said quietly.

'You've got absolutely no reason to be jealous,' he insisted.

'I'm not jealous,' she maintained. But she was. All this evening she'd felt them drawing closer, but there was still a long way to go. Rob had only explained about Susan because he'd had to. Was that because she didn't particularly matter, or because she did—and now he was feeling guilty?

He didn't say much on the way home; just things like did she want the heater turned up and the odd muttered exclamation about some of the reckless driving they encountered.

'I dare say most of them are drunk,' said Jenna, falling into line. She desperately wanted to ask him more about Susan, but couldn't manage it. She knew it was silly when Rob had made it so clear how he felt about her herself. Well, it was up to him. Presumably he'd tell her in his own good time. If there was anything to tell.

'You've been very quiet all the way home, Jenna,' said Rob when he had parked the car in its usual place.

'I—didn't want to distract you with all those madmen on the road,' she pretended.

'How thoughtful you are,' he said warmly.

'I like to think so. Rob——'

'Yes, Jenna?'

If only he'd called her Pixie, she might have managed to voice her fears, but he hadn't. 'I just wanted to thank you very much for giving me such a wonderful birthday treat.'

'It *was* a good evening, was it not?' he asked as though he also needed reassurance.

'The best I've had for a very long time,' she was able to tell him truthfully.

'Then it's all been worthwhile,' he said, leaning over to kiss her with a sort of sad desperation.

Earlier, she had imagined them ending the evening locked in steamy embraces on the sitting-room couch—if not actually in bed. But when they got into the house, Rob said, 'I suppose I'd better ring old Porteous in case anything serious happened tonight.'

'I suppose so,' Jenna echoed reluctantly. 'Well, thanks again, Rob. It was wonderful.' She moved towards the stairs, looking back at him wistfully. Surely he'd tell her the call would only take a minute, and then——

'It was nothing. I'd give you the moon if I could,' he said in an odd, dry sort of voice, before going into the dining-room and shutting the door.

CHAPTER EIGHT

IT WAS Monday morning and Jenna was out on her rounds while Rob took surgery. She had just told Rosie Meldrum, that redoutable old warrior in the quayside cottage on the other side of the harbour that she would have to go to hospital.

'Havers! Ye can jest see to me here,' declared Rosie confidently. 'They're saying in the town that ye're awful clever.'

'Not clever enough to cope with this, Mrs Meldrum. Your leg is badly burned and you've lost a lot of skin. It'll need grafting eventually, but meanwhile you must rest it completely. And that's not possible at home.'

'The neighbours'll see tae ma food and that.'

'Not this time. I know how much you hate the idea, but this time you've got to go. I know that Dr William would say so too.'

'I'm no' going.' Rosie lay back in her box bed, arms folded, defying Jenna to argue further.

Monday was always the busiest day of the week and Jenna was already running late. There was only one thing to be done. She went back to Harbour House and put the problem to William. 'She *must* go to hospital,' she said earnestly when she'd explained what had befallen old Rosie this time. 'Extensive second and third degree burns, William. I've done her up with temporary dressings, but a leg like that should really be open to the air. And those cats of hers sleep on her bed. I can't see her shooing them off, can you?'

William said she was absolutely right. 'I'll go and see if I can persuade her,' he said.

'I'll drive you—but you mustn't get excited. I only hope that Rob doesn't kill me when he finds out what I've encouraged you to do.'

'He'll understand that we had no alternative,' he said, already quite excited at the thought of doing something useful.

He managed to persuade Rosie by promising that she should come home again if she didn't like hospital. 'Craven of me, I know,' he said to Jenna as she drove him home. 'But I'm relying on the sister in charge of the burns unit to keep Rosie in. She's a Port Lindsay girl and they know each other well.'

'What a blessing,' murmured Jenna. Having seen him safely inside, she returned to Rosie's cottage to wait for the ambulance. Rosie was quite capable of cancelling it if she changed her mind.

'You're very late, Doctor,' said Mrs MacKenzie-Smith severely when Jenna got to her at last.

'An emergency,' said Jenna briefly. 'A serious accident and the patient needing hospital treatment. So what's the trouble today, Mrs Smith?'

'My name is *MacKenzie*-Smith and I've already explained to the receptionist that I have nasty pains in my stomach.'

Not her stomach exactly. Jenna examined her, though not without protest, and found her whole abdomen hard and distended. She asked the obvious question. 'When did you last have your bowels open?'

The patient's expression showed her outrage at so indelicate a query. 'Two days—three?' prompted Jenna firmly.

The patient averted her eyes. 'Perhaps—a week. . . One does not count.'

One does if one is wise, thought Jenna grimly. 'I'm afraid you've got an obstruction in your colon,' she said tactfully. 'And that is a hospital matter.'

'Surely you could give me something. Castor oil?'

Jenna didn't like to think of the result of that. 'That's not what you need,' she said patiently. 'You need to go to hospital. May I use your phone?'

Permitted by a queenly nod, Jenna dialled ambulance control and prepared to be bawled out for poor organisation. They'd be furious at having to send two fully manned ambulances to Port Lindsay in the one morning. Then, as there was nobody else to do it, Jenna packed a suitcase before persuading the next-door neighbour to look out for the ambulance and make sure the house was locked up afterwards. If she stayed to see another patient safely away, she'd never finish her calls in time for the special diagnostic session at three.

Praying for no more emergencies, Jenna headed for her next assignment: an elderly husband and wife precariously poised on the brink between sheltered housing and residential care. They were in their late eighties and touchingly devoted. Jenna went over them both before writing their repeat prescriptions He had long-standing arthritis and she moderately severe angina. After that, she rang the social work department and begged for their home help assistance to be stepped up, persuaded a doubtful warden that they were coping and then heated up a can of soup for their lunch. Somehow, they must be kept together. Parting would kill them.

Just the one visit now, to Farmer Caird up country. He had developed severe gastro-enteritis last Friday, but should be improving nicely by now; ready for solids and a bit of activity, though not up to a day's work yet. . .

'Yes, of course I'll look at your son while I'm here, Mr Caird. Fell and struck his head, you say? When was this? This morning? What a good thing I was coming then.' Oh, please—not another hospital case!

Jenna examined the boy. 'He's got a very nasty bruise but there's no serious damage. As you say, the sofa obviously broke his fall. Still, a lad his age shouldn't be falling over for no apparent reason all the time and I want to give him a thorough going over. Could you bring him to the surgery one afternoon?'

'Well, now.' He looked as worried as though he'd been asked to visit the moon. 'The wife goes to the supermarket on a Thursday. . .'

'Thursday it is then, as long as she can get him to me by three.'

'Two would mebbe suit her better. Are you sure ye cannae look him over here?'

'Quite sure, Mr Caird. Some of the equipment I shall need is not portable.' And, more to the point, he'll not answer my questions fully with you going on at him to pull himself together!

The appointment agreed to, Jenna hurried out to her car, glancing at her watch as she went. One-thirty already. Goodbye lunch if she didn't step on it.

Mrs Cullen had left her lunch on the kitchen table. Soup in a flask, a cheese sandwich and an apple. She knew better than to leave Jenna to fend for herself after the roasting Rob had given her the last time she did it.

Jenna poured the soup into the waiting mug. It was barely warm. Never mind, she'd be able to drink it the sooner. She was finishing it when Rob came in. 'Where the hell have you been?' he demanded. He looked angry and she assumed he objected to her taking William to Rosie's.

'I knew you wouldn't like it, but I had no choice, Rob. She would never have gone for me.'

'I don't know what you're talking about,' he said.

'Rosie Meldrum.'

'What about her?'

'Didn't William tell you? Obviously not.' Jenna explained and Rob said he'd probably have done the same.

'So why are you angry, then?' she wondered.

'I'm not angry—just very worried. There was talk in the chemist's of an accident to a red VW like yours on the Forfar road. And when you didn't come in for lunch—anyway, you obviously weren't involved. You've got too much to do, though, coming in at this time.'

'Not really, but with two patients for hospital in the one morning, I got rather behind.'

'You've got too much to do,' he repeated.

'Surely not. Your parents managed, didn't they? Just the two of them?'

'It's a long time since those days and they had an assistant for the last three years of Mother's life. They had to, after all the new houses were built.'

'I didn't know that.'

'There's so much you still don't know, Jenna. One of these—yes, what is it, Mrs Cullen?' he asked irritably when she came in.

She blinked, offended at the non-use of her Christian name, and darting Jenna a glance of blame. 'I'm very sorry to have to interrupt, Doctors,' she said elaborately, 'but there's a boy at the surgery door with a badly cut hand. It's bleeding a lot.'

'I'll go,' they said in unison.

'Finish your lunch,' ordered Rob, dashing off. Yet another brief encounter and yesterday had been just as bad.

Jenna finished her lunch, checking her day book as she ate. Only two more calls to make, so if Rob wasn't too busy, they might manage to meet for tea. William would be there too, but at least she would *see* Rob. It was something to look forward to.

Jenna was crossing the road to her car when William came to the front door and called her back. 'Phone, Jenna.'

She let a huge refrigerated fish truck thunder past, then ran back across the road. 'Who is it?' she asked, going up the steps.

'I didn't recognise the voice,' said William. 'Anyway, it's not a patient—they're on the private line.'

'Man or woman?' asked Jenna guardedly, though surely not even Jake would——

'A woman with a heavy cold,' supplied William. 'She sounded as though she was talking through her hankie.'

A patient after all, then, but why the private line? And how did she know the number? Jenna picked up the phone. 'Hello, Dr Fielding speaking.'

There was quite a pause before the woman said awkwardly, 'I'd like to see you, please.' Her voice sounded clear enough now.

'Why? Who are you?' Jenna asked, puzzled.

Another pause before she said, 'I need to consult you. Professionally. Without anybody knowing. And I can't come to the surgery.'

'You want a house call, then,' said Jenna, supposing her to be disabled.

'Yes—please.'

'Very well. Now if you'll just tell me your name and address——'

'Oh, dear. Yes, of course.' Had she really thought that wouldn't be necessary? 'Lindsay Mains Farm,' she whispered. 'Susan MacArthur.'

When she'd taken that in, Jenna asked sharply, 'Are you sure this is a professional matter?'

'I'm sure all right,' Susan said bitterly. 'I only wish I weren't!'

'And you're registered with this practice?'

'Yes, unfortunately.'

More and more peculiar. What *did* she want that had to be kept so secret? Secret enough to oblige her to disguise her voice from William? Yet she was clearly in distress. Wondering what she was letting herself in for, Jenna asked, 'Will about four this afternoon suit?'

'Perfect. At least——' Again that tone of bitterness. 'I'll expect you then—and thanks.' She rang off.

Jenna went to the surgery to get Susan's records. She could understand her not wanting to consult Rob and with William temporarily out of action, that left only her. But why the embarrassment and insistence on secrecy? Why couldn't she come to the surgery in the normal way? I hope she isn't planning to do away with me, Jenna thought wryly. I can just see the headlines. 'Slighted Woman Slays Rival in Fit of Jealous Rage.' I wonder if I should leave a note to say where I'm going?

She didn't, of course. She had promised Susan confidentiality and she'd honour that promise. All the same, if she offers me anything to eat or drink, I'll refuse, Jenna decided as she set off.

The first two calls were merely routine checks on housebound ninety-year-olds and soon Jenna was heading west towards Lindsay Mains, in plenty of time for this mysterious appointment.

Susan opened the door herself. She looked pale and tense and Jenna hardly recognised the vibrant beauty she'd seen at the Lobster Pot with Rob. 'Thank you for coming,' she said formally, adding, 'Everybody's out.'

Jenna frowned as she asked, 'Is that significant?'

'Of course. The fewer people who know about this, the better.' She led the way to the stairs.

'Surely we can talk down here,' said Jenna firmly, not moving from the doormat.

'You can't examine me in the hall,' returned Susan testily.

So she was ill. 'What's the trouble?' asked Jenna in her professional voice, but Susan didn't answer until they were in her bedroom and she had closed the door. Even then, she took her time. 'My father keeps me very short of money and checks every damn last penny, so I can't go privately. I tried Dr Morrison in St Fergus further down the coast, but he said he couldn't do anything for me until I'd changed to his list, and that would take too long. You're my only hope,' she ended despairingly.

She looked so desperate that the doctor in Jenna took over. 'My dear girl, whatever is the matter?' she asked sympathetically.

'I'm pregnant,' said Susan.

Jenna felt her knees giving way and she clutched at a chest of drawers for support. 'My God!' she breathed. 'Are you sure?'

'Oh, I'm sure. I've missed twice now, so I got a testing kit when I went to Forfar with Dad for the cattle sales. There's no doubt.'

Jenna strove to get a grip. Six—or possibly seven weeks. Before Rob and I met. . . 'And you're sure you did the test properly?'

'Yes. It was quite easy. Anyway, you'll be able to tell, will you not?'

'Ye-es. . .' She was being so feeble; had to get a

grip. Somehow, Jenna got herself across to the bed and threw back the duvet. 'Right, take off your things.' Now Jenna, open your case and wash your hands and put on disposable gloves. . .

'Well?' asked Susan when Jenna had finished.

Jenna nodded in confirmation. 'Have you told—him? The father?' She couldn't bring herself to say Rob's name.

'He wouldn't want to know.'

Jenna could believe that. But she must say the right things. Ask the right questions. 'I think you should tell him.'

'I want you to arrange an abortion.' She sounded very determined.

'It's not that simple——' I'm not handling this well; I'm not in charge. Too upset. . . Jenna made a supreme effort. 'You're probably no more than seven weeks pregnant, so there's time to think this thing through. You really ought to discuss it with—the father. He may be more supportive than you expect.' That's more like it. Forget the implications for you. Be professional. She's your patient. You accepted her when you agreed to come.

'I tell you he wouldn't want to know.' Susan was even more positive now. 'Look, Dr Fielding, there's no way I can have this child, even if I wanted it—which I don't. . .' She choked on the last words and her face worked pitifully for a few seconds before she said quite firmly, 'I must have an abortion.'

'I can arrange an early hospital appointment for you, but I still think you should talk it over with——' Jenna's turn to swallow hard now '—your lover. Why should you have all the trouble and worry?'

'I'm sure you mean well, but I know it wouldn't do any good.' At the sound of wheels on gravel, Susan leapt off the bed as if stung and grabbed her clothes. 'My father—back already. He mustn't see you here.' She gave up the effort of dressing and reached for a bath robe. 'Quick! Down the back stairs!'

'He'll have seen my car,' Jenna pointed out.

'Oh, God, so he will!' She seemed genuinely afraid.

Light footsteps on the stairs and a girl's voice calling. 'My sister,' breathed Susan. 'But don't tell her. For heaven's sake, don't tell *her*!'

'Don't worry.' Jenna repacked her case. 'Just a minor tummy upset,' she said when Shelagh opened the door and demanded to be told what was wrong. 'Nothing to worry about. I'll be in touch very soon to find out how you're progressing,' she told Susan as she stumbled out of the room, leaving the sisters together.

She drove away in a daze. Get away from the house, off MacArthur land and find a quiet spot for a think.

On the first straight stretch of road, Jenna eased the car up on to the grass verge and switched off the headlights. She was trembling violently with the effort of playing the doctor, when all she'd wanted to do was to shriek aloud her own hurt and despair.

Susan must have conceived before I came to Port Lindsay. But does that make it any better? Not really, although it explains Rob's attitude; loving one minute and hanging back the next. I think I knew they were more than friends; just didn't want to believe. . .

Susan will think better of her decision to go it alone when she's calmed down. And if she tells her sister, then Shelagh will insist that Rob is told, and Rob. . . this is probably all that's needed to make him choose between us. Oh, Rob! And I'd thought you were so honest and strong. Not even Jake, with all his affairs, has begotten a child.

Why did I tell Shelagh that Susan had a tummy

upset? Why couldn't I have said she'd strained her back or something? Shelagh will soon worm the truth out of her. She knows they're lovers. That's why she came to warn me off. Jenna leaned back, gazing wearily round the car. She caught sight of the clock. Ten past five; she was going to be late for evening surgery. You'll need to get a move on. You'll need to wash your face. It's probably got mascara all over it.

'Not too many for a change,' observed Meg brightly when she saw Jenna, who had crept in via the surgery door to avoid the men.

Jenna hurried by, head averted. 'Great! Just give me five minutes to tidy up and then I'll buzz.'

In the consulting room, she eyed herself in the mirror over the washbasin. She looked as though she'd seen a ghost, but, that apart, there was nothing a wet tissue couldn't cope with. Dispose of a smudge or two and run a comb through your hair. You'll do. Nobody expects a doctor to look glamorous.

Jenna had seen three patients by the time Rob looked in. 'At my post, as you see,' she said in a voice like brittle glass.

'I know, Meg told me. I only came to see if you were all right.' He eyed her closely. 'You look completely washed out, Jenna.'

'I'm all right,' she insisted. 'Why wouldn't I be?' After all, this isn't the first time I've been deceived by a man!

'You've had such a tiring day.'

'No doubt you have too. Now you have to excuse me. I've a phone call to make before my next patient,' she invented.

'You're terribly on edge, dear. Let me finish off for you,' he urged.

'Oh, do stop fussing!' she exploded. 'I'm perfectly capable of doing my own work—if I'm allowed to!'

He recoiled as though she'd struck him. 'I don't doubt that, but surely, a little help——'

'I've said it before and I'll say it again. There'd be none of this if I were a man. I can cope perfectly well if you'll just stop pestering me!'

'You'll explain that,' he said tightly.

'Gladly!' And what a big lie that was when to explain was the last thing she wanted. She picked up the phone as though to dial.

It looked as if Rob was going to snatch it out of her hand when Miss Wilma Smith came in. 'Right after surgery!' he hissed, daring her to refuse.

Jenna ignored him and fussed her patient into a chair. 'Now tell me exactly how you've been this past week,' she invited rashly as she replaced the phone.

The recital took some time and all of Jenna's powers of concentration, when her mind would keep straying to her own problems.

'But all in all, I'd say it's the knee that's bothering me most right now,' Wilma summarised at last.

'I'm sure,' agreed Jenna. 'When you banged it on that chair you damaged the protective bursa—that is, the soft pad over the kneecap. They called it housemaids' knee in the days when there were housemaids. It'll feel much easier when I've put on a pressure bandage and it should settle in a few days.' She paused. 'I don't know what to suggest though for that dog next door, left alone and barking all day. I suppose you could try the Council or the RSPCA.' Another pause. 'Of course, if you were out more yourself, it wouldn't be such an annoyance.'

Wilma said she'd thought of that, had gone to the

Bingo yesterday afternoon and might look in at the Church coffee morning next Saturday.

A breakthrough, thought Jenna. A dog had succeeded where medical expertise had failed. 'What a good idea,' she said, nearly adding that it was indeed an ill wind that did nobody any good.

Not that I can take much comfort from that proverb, she reflected grimly, as she watched Wilma limp out almost happily with her bandaged knee and a repeat prescription for anti-depressants.

Before seeing the last patient, Jenna slipped through to the kitchen to tell Mrs Cullen that she wouldn't be wanting supper. 'I have to go out again and may be some time. I wouldn't want you to have the bother of keeping it hot,' she explained.

Mrs Cullen nodded, accepting such consideration as her due. She'd whipped Jenna's cutlery off the table almost before she was out of the room.

Ten minutes to check the lifeboat engineer, pronounce his chest clear after his post-influenzal infection and warn him not to be so slow to see a doctor another time. Then Jenna could call it a day. She put on her coat and went out by the surgery door. As Rob was on call that night, there was no need to leave a message.

She crossed the road and walked along the quayside, glancing down into the oily water of the harbour, lit fitfully by the street lights; listening to the lazy slap of water against the hulls as the boats shifted gently at their moorings. All was quiet, but it wouldn't be long before the fishermen went aboard to prepare for sea at the end of the compulsory tie-up days. The forecast was poor, but they'd put out anyway, braving storms and danger. The luxury to choose their time was denied them by faceless bureaucrats who'd probably take taxis in a shower, rather than sully their beautifully furled brollies.

Opposite the Lobster Pot, Jenna crossed the road. There was hardly anybody there tonight, but Nick was at his usual table, eating alone with a book propped open in front of him. Suddenly Jenna felt ashamed of seeking him out after all the excuses she'd made of late not to see him, but he'd already looked up when the door creaked shut behind her. 'Jenna—over here,' he called just as though they'd planned this meeting.

'Nick—how nice,' she responded. 'Just so long as you're not expecting anybody.'

'Madonna did promise to look in, but I'm thinking she was too busy,' he returned with a grin, having leapt up to pull out a chair for her.

She looked at his plate. 'That fish looks very good—I'll have the same, please,' she told the hovering waitress.

'To what do I owe this unexpected pleasure?' Nick asked curiously. 'Has old Ma Cullen been trying to poison you?'

'Not yet, though I sometimes wonder if it's only a question of time,' Jenna answered. 'I think she resents the assistants staying in the house.'

'Only if they're women,' said Nick. 'She's terrified that either Rob or his father will remarry and send her packing.'

So he did know about Isobel, then. Why had he never mentioned her? Not that it or anything else would make any difference now. Jenna sighed without realising it and Nick asked if she'd had a really rotten day.

'Not much worse than usual,' she returned bravely.

'They work you too hard, Jenna. Why do you put up with it?'

'Right now, they don't have any choice, with William on the sick list,' she answered fairly. 'We've put out feelers for a locum, but so far there haven't been any replies.'

'That doesn't surprise me,' said Nick. 'I'd not be here in this dead-and-alive hole myself if I hadn't been handed a lucrative practice on a plate. Do you think you'll stick it?'

It was too good a chance to pass up. 'I'm not sure,' said Jenna slowly as though there really was some doubt. 'The work is as interesting and varied as I'd get anywhere, but I'm a townie at heart. I'm more than half inclined to pack it in at the end of my probationary three months.' I did that well, she thought.

'That'd be a great disappointment to me,' said Nick firmly. He chased a final chip around his plate. 'To Rob too. The whisper is that he's fallen in love with you.'

Jenna was very glad that the waitress brought her supper at that moment. She made quite a business of saying thank you and asking for a glass of white wine. Then she turned to Nick with a carefully prepared smile of mild amusement. 'Then for heaven's sake do me a favour and whisper back that there's no truth in it. I can do without the whole MacArthur clan on my back for poaching!'

Nick smiled broadly back. 'Of course I'm very glad to hear that, but if that's the case, why did you let him take you to Lindsay Castle last Saturday?'

'Does the local Mafia never sleep?' wondered Jenna. 'Actually that was—it was William's doing,' she said, inspired. 'He'd intended to take me himself—for my birthday—but he didn't feel up to it, so Rob had to take me.'

'And hated every moment of it,' Nick suggested derisively.

'I hope not. Anyway he was very good about it.

Though I gather that Susan wasn't too pleased.' And now please *please* stop probing before I burst into tears and give the whole show away!

'I'll bet!' exclaimed Nick, his telepathic sense definitely out of order. 'She's been angling for Rob ever since Dougal Donaldson ditched her to marry Shelagh.'

That wasn't quite the way Shelagh had told it. 'Did he really? Then it's a wonder the girls are such friends.'

'I wonder if they are,' mused Nick. 'Shelagh was always her father's pet and, according to my grandfather, he's never made any secret of that. And he's never forgiven poor old Sue for not being a boy.'

'Then it's about time somebody explained to that silly old man that it's basically fathers who are responsible for the sex of their children, whether they like it or not,' Jenna returned mechanically, from her specialised knowledge. 'I'm surprised she stayed at home, if that's how things were.'

'That was largely the mother's doing. She was never well after Susan was born and the poor lass was made to feel guilty about that as well. Especially as her mother wasn't allowed to try for the son so desperately wanted.'

'But surely, once her mother died. . .' In any other circumstances she'd be feeling really sorry for Susan.

'By then Rob was on the scene,' said Nick. 'Do eat up, Jenna, I'm dying to try the plum cobbler.'

'After fried fish? You must have the digestion of an ox. Just you carry on and I'll catch up in time for coffee,' returned Jenna, relieved at the way she'd managed to turn the conversation. Impossible not to feel sorry for the girl she wanted to hate for being the one to dash her own hopes of happiness. But Jenna was honest and she had to admit that Rob was just as much to blame as Susan was. 'Oh, hell,' she muttered on a sob.

'Have you swallowed a bone?' asked Nick, noting her watery eyes.

'Yes.' She coughed elaborately. 'I'll just go—see if I can dislodge it.' Jenna fled to the ladies' to fight for control in private. Nick must never suspect the truth. If he did, the careful smokescreen she'd laid earlier would all be wasted.

When she returned to the table, she was ready with a tale about a patient in Casualty whom she'd treated for a peanut stuck in the trachea. 'By a miracle, it flew out when I upended him and thumped his back,' she said. 'Otherwise it would have meant a bronchoscopy.'

'I'm very glad he was spared that—whatever it is,' said Nick, making a face. 'No, spare me an explanation—it would put me off my pudding. Really, you doctors!'

So they talked of less off-putting things for the rest of the meal. Such things as holidays and sailing, and Nick revealed that he owned a twelve-footer. 'It's a pity you're not staying on,' he sighed. 'You'd enjoy sailing. I know you would.'

'I'm sure I would,' she allowed, 'but, as I said earlier, I'm a townie. What wouldn't I give to hear a good symphony concert. Or go to a play. . .' She sounded so pathetic that he offered to take her to Aberdeen the next time the Royal Scottish Orchestra visited the city.

'But you don't like classical music, Nick,' she remembered.

'Anything for a pretty girl,' he said with a comical leer.

Jenna preened and smirked and told him he was a real caution. They flirted outrageously until closing time, causing the barman to say as they left that that

Dr Fielding was a right one for the men and he wouldn't mind a turn in the queue himself.

Nick walked Jenna home. Every window of Harbour House was in darkness, but then it was after midnight. On the doorstep, he kissed her. Getting no response worth the trouble, he said, 'Were you telling the truth earlier—about you and Rob?'

She dodged that by saying she'd broken with a man she'd been with for a long time, just before coming to Port Lindsay. 'And I'm not over it yet. That's all.'

'That explains a lot,' he said. 'Why didn't you tell me before?'

'Because it's not something to brag about,' she returned truthfully.

'Poor wee Jenna!' He kissed her again, but as a friend this time. 'We'll go out again very soon, huh?'

'Yes, please. It was a lovely evening, Nick.' And much better than having that threatened showdown with Rob, she acknowledged, when she'd finally persuaded Nick that the evening was over. It would come, of course. Unless Susan took her advice and told Rob about the baby. Either way, she'd be in better shape to cope after a good night's sleep; something a couple of Mogadon should ensure. Jenna bolted the front door and headed for the stairs. She was suddenly, unbearably weary.

As soon as she switched on the light by her bed, Rob came out of the shadows and stationed himself in the archway, blocking her escape.

'Oh, no,' she breathed. 'Please, not now. I'm much too tired.'

'What, no old chesnut about having a headache?' he asked harshly. He'd misunderstood her protest as he'd misunderstood so much else she'd said to him. 'But you needn't worry. I'm not here to make love to you, but to clear the air—and by God, it needs clearing.'

Jenna gave a brief hysterical laugh at such irony. 'You never spoke a truer word,' she heard herself say in a high, artificial voice.

'You're drunk,' Rob accused scornfully.

'I certainly am not,' she retorted. 'But if it's possible to misunderstand, you'll always manage it! No wonder we're continually at odds.'

'So it's all my fault—as usual. Whatever it is *this* time,' he said bitterly.

'Absolutely!' she snapped back, because if anything was true, that was.

'Then spell it out!' he commanded.

Jenna gazed at him; at his furrowed brow and what she'd certainly have read as genuine perplexity in his deepset blue eyes but for that visit to Susan. 'I—I. . .' But what was there to say? 'Couldn't this wait until morning?' she pleaded. 'I'm too tired.'

'Are you, now? Then how come you were laughing on the doorstep with Nick Lawson not five minutes since? You didn't sound too tired then. Or is tiredness only a feeling you have when you're with me?'

'You're the one who's kept on all day about me overdoing things.'

'And all I got for my concern was a feminist blast about not being treated like a man!'

He'd provided as good an excuse as any for the final quarrel, when the real trouble was too deep, and not hers to mention.

'Play it down if you must,' she said, 'but the fact remains that you've never given me equal status. And in the end—well, I just blew up. As anybody would.'

'End—what end?' he demanded. 'I've lost count of the number of times you've accused me of the same thing. You were friendly enough at lunchtime today, but you practically bit my head off the next time we met. And I want to know why!'

'I've told you,' she insisted. 'I've told you over and over. And unless you treat me as an equal, I'll—I'll. . . And I've been thinking. It's a great mistake to be—to be too friendly, as well as working together. We should never have tried. It's only made a bad situation worse. And I'm going when my three months are up.'

'What a load of rubbish!' snarled Rob. 'I don't believe a word of it. There's something else behind this—something that must have happened this afternoon. And I mean to know what!'

He took a step towards her and Jenna retreated two. 'Jake!' she cried wildly. 'I've talked to Jake. I'm going back to him!'

She couldn't have hit on anything more effective. Rob stopped short, gasping with shock. Then Jenna had to watch helplessly while his expression changed from anger to utter disgust. 'You nasty, deceitful little hypocrite!' he sneered bitingly. 'And to think I believed you—bled for you—when you told me that tale of his treatment of you. You're two of a kind and you deserve each other!' He turned and stumbled blindly out of the room, not caring about the noise he made knocking over a chair and slamming the door. Moments later, she heard his own door open and shut, then silence.

Jenna collapsed limply on to her bed. She'd done it—and in the worst possible way. She knew she had to end it; had known ever since Susan's confession. Because what Rob had learned to feel for her in a few short weeks would count as nothing beside his years with Susan—especially when she told him she was carrying his child. Yes, she'd had to end it, but had she had to paint herself so badly in the process? Hadn't she been hurt enough?

CHAPTER NINE

'MY, BUT you're quick off the mark the day,' Meg said admiringly when she and Jenna met in the passage next morning. 'You're getting just like Dr Rob.'

Jenna could have done without a compliment like that. 'Just one or two things to be done before I start,' she mumbled. Like arranging Susan's hospital appointment without anybody overhearing.

'Right! Give me a buzz when you're ready for your first patient, then,' said Meg, unaware of anything wrong. In the dim light of the passage, she hadn't noticed how white and drawn Jenna was. Not that it would have mattered. Jenna could always have waffled on about night duty.

There had been just the one call: to the council sheltered housing complex. The warden had found her oldest resident wandering in her nightie and decided she had the excuse she wanted to get her out of the place. Jenna had scotched that by saying that everybody was allowed a lapse or two before being officially labelled senile, but it had been touch and go.

Going into the consulting room, she slipped the bolt. She couldn't risk Meg coming in while she was making Susan's appointment. Of course there was nobody in Appointments yet. She should have foreseen that. Write the consultant's letter then, making out the best possible case for a termination. Single girl, afraid of domineering father, highly emotional. Better not mention that she was twenty-six, though. Girls of that age didn't stay at home any more if they weren't happy there.

Jenna tried the hospital again and got through this time. Then she wrote a note to Susan, telling her about her appointment for today week at ten-thirty. She couldn't risk the phone. One crossed line and it'd be all round Port Lindsay before nightfall that Susan MacArthur was pregnant by Dr Rob.

When Meg tapped on the door and tried the handle, Jenna leapt to open it. 'Just wondered if you were, ready, Doctor,' said Meg. 'Only the natives are getting restless.'

'I'm as ready as I'll ever be,' said Jenna with a thin little smile.

That morning, she saw three patients who needed detailed examinations, and arranged to see them the following afternoon. So bang goes my half-day, she thought, when she'd told the last one four o'clock. Meg brought Jenna a cup of coffee with her list of visits. While drinking it, she juggled her calls so as to be late for lunch and avoid Rob. He must have done the same, though, and they arrived back only minutes apart. Jenna wondered if she could carry her lunch through to the surgery on the pretext of letters to write, but William was waiting to eat with them both, all unaware of trouble.

It was a difficult meal, with William in a chatty mood and asking questions of them both. Jenna managed fairly well, but Rob made no effort at all. When William said he'd never known him so quiet, Rob said he had things on his mind. He looked at Jenna as he spoke and she wondered whether Susan had taken her advice and told him.

'Is it something I could help with?' his father asked sympathetically.

Rob pretended to be immersed in a difficult diagnosis and they discussed that for a while. Then William suggested asking for Jenna's opinion.

She declined, saying she had little experience of orthopaedic conditions. Rob said he wasn't surprised; it was an unsuitable speciality for women. Jenna lifted her chin and said some women felt that way about men in gynaecology, and William, with the worst possible timing, said anybody would think they didn't like one another from the way they talked.

'I can't think why,' said Rob tonelessly, getting up and going out.

William watched his exit, frowning. 'He really is down about something today,' he said. 'Any ideas, Jenna?'

She shrugged. 'I know he's disappointed that there haven't been any replies to the advertisement for a locum and with Dr Porteous unwilling to do more than the occasional evening. . .' She shrugged again.

'I'm sure I could——' he began and she told him certainly not. That would only compound Rob's worries. . . 'You'll do as you're told,' she ended firmly.

It was while she was doing her afternoon house calls that it occurred to Jenna how much easier it would be to cope with her private miseries if she and Rob weren't under the same roof. She would ask Nick to recommend a small cottage to rent. He must know of one when, in Scotland, lawyers dealt with nearly all property transactions. She missed her teabreak, dropping into Nick's office instead. 'Are you quite sure the owners won't mind?' she asked when she'd settled on number four, Quayside Row, several doors down from Rosie. It was a holiday house.

'Mind? They'll be thrilled,' he said confidently.

'They're always on at me to find them some winter lets, to keep the place aired if nothing else.'

Telling William was the worst bit. There was no way she could avoid hurting his feelings. 'I don't know whether or not you've noticed,' she began, 'but Mrs Cullen and I just don't hit it off. So I think it'd be best if I moved out.'

He refused to hear of it, saying that he would speak to Jeannie. She persuaded him not to, saying that they'd never get another housekeeper as good if she took offence and left.

William said he'd no idea things were as bad as that. 'Rob'll not like this,' he said positively.

If there was one thing Jenna was sure of it was that Rob would be very relieved—especially when Susan told him her news. She'd come to regard that as certain. 'I'm sure he'll understand when I explain,' she said soothingly, and William said how good it was to know how much better they were getting on these days.

Jenna let that go by too. With a storm threatening to break over Harbour House at any moment, she wouldn't be making any waves.

Jenna managed to squeeze in a look at the cottage during her house calls next morning. It was very small, but comfortable and appropriately furnished, and she arranged with Nick to move in the following day. 'Just think of all the cosy evenings we'll have, now you're moving out of barracks,' he said, putting his arms round her and pulling her close.

In her anxiety to get out from under Rob's feet, this was a complication she hadn't foreseen. 'Unless we get that locum soon, there'll be precious few cosy moments for anybody,' she said, freeing herself. 'We're heading for a flu epidemic.' Four new cases hardly added up to an epidemic, but life was complicated enough without Nick trying to start something.

'You live for your work,' he grumbled.

'I certainly couldn't live without it,' she countered briskly. 'Now I'm off to give Nanny Cullen the good news that she'll soon be rid of me.'

At Harbour House, she found Rob hovering in the hall with a face like thunder. 'I thought this was supposed to be your half-day,' he growled before she'd even got the door shut.

Jenna took her time about removing her coat, waiting for her heart rate to slow down before risking speech. 'Is there a problem?' she got out eventually.

'There is. I have two patients coming in this afternoon and now Meg tells me you've booked in three of yours.'

'Yours weren't down in the book.'

He had to admit that. 'But knowing it was your half-day, I didn't see the need.'

'So of course the muddle is my fault—as usual.'

'Don't be childish!' he snarled.

'If anybody around here needs to grow up, it's you, Rob Strachan!' Jenna snarled back. 'And I don't just mean professionally.' Heavens, that had been risky!

But Rob was too strung up to pursue that last bit. 'Never mind the insults,' he said through his teeth, 'how are we going to resolve this mess?'

'You have the consulting room and I'll manage in the dispensary,' she said. 'Fortunately, that old examination couch has never been removed.'

'There isn't room in there to swing a cat!'

'As I don't propose to whirl my patients round at arm's length, that is not a problem,' Jenna returned smartly.

Rob swallowed visibly, striving for control. 'Since

the mix-up is largely my fault, you can have the consulting room and I'll take the dispensary.'

'That's just not practical,' said Jenna. 'The dispensary is tiny and you are not. *I'll* use it. After all, I'm no bigger than a pixie.'

He recoiled as though she had hit him. 'My God, you really know how to put the boot in,' he gasped, the pain visible in his eyes, if she cared to see it. But, in saying that, she'd hurt herself quite as much as Rob.

'Yes, I've learned a lot since coming here,' she whispered unsteadily. 'You're—an excellent teacher.' Then unable to risk another word, Jenna fled upstairs and didn't come down again until she was sure that lunch was over.

The afternoon was awkward to say the least. Jenna had to go several times to the consulting room for instruments and Rob kept coming to the dispensary for drugs, splints and so on. The patients thought it was wonderful, and Jenna's last one summed up for them all. 'To think of you doctors going to all this trouble for us,' she said. 'You could teach those old ministers a thing or two, I'm thinking.'

Jenna paused, opthalmoscope in hand. 'Sorry, I'm not with you, Mrs McKechnie.' She was thinking of churchmen.

'Those old ones trying to run the Health Service,' explained the patient. 'Have ye not seen our new hospital yet? Gey great entrance hall like an airport lounge. What a waste of space! And here's you and Dr Rob carrying on in a cupboard!'

What a speech, but obviously meant as a tribute. Jenna agreed that it took a medical person to establish priorities, since that seemed to be what Mrs McKechnie was saying.

'Exactly! They should make that Lord Dr Owen

Minister of Health instead of letting him waste his time on politics. Why are you examining my eyes, Doctor?' she asked with a bewildering change of direction. 'I've only come about being tired and short of breath.'

'There are lots of reasons for that and I need to find the right one.'

'You mean that if your eyes are bad, it can make you short of breath?'

'Not exactly, Mrs McKechnie, but I'll explain fully just as soon as I've diagnosed your problem.' And with your weird perception of the way the human body works, my dear, that's not something I'll find very easy. She laid aside the opthalmoscope to take another look at the scar on her patient's forearm, so thick and white and coarse. The typical keloid scar of sarcoidosis. Add that to the fatigue, the shortage of breath, the rash. . . 'You've been so patient,' said Jenna at last, 'but I've finished for now. I'd like you to come tomorrow morning so that I can take a blood sample and I'll also be making you an appointment to have some X-rays. After that, we'll know for sure what we're dealing with.' Jenna would also like to refer her to a recognised expert in the field, so she went through to the house, to ask William for a name.

Only Rob was there, lounging back in his chair and gazing broodingly into the fire with the tea-tray untouched beside him.

'Sorry, I was looking for your father,' Jenna said awkwardly.

He turned and looked at her sorrowfully. 'He's lying down. Is it urgent?'

'No. . .' But she might as well ask him. 'I just want to know where to find the nearest specialist in sarcoidosis.'

His professional interest was aroused. 'Sarcoid—that's very rare. Who is it?'

At least he hadn't questioned her diagnosis. 'Flora McKechnie of Fisher Wynd. Of course I haven't got X-rays or a white cell count yet, but the signs are all there.' She outlined her findings.

'I wish I'd seen her,' he said.

Jenna bristled. 'Do you want me to make her an appointment with you, then?'

'Of course not! I only meant for interest's sake.' He paused. 'Dr Bruce in Aberdeen is probably the nearest authority.'

'And which hospital is he attached to?' asked Jenna.

A thin smile flitted briefly across Rob's rugged features. 'A note to the Department of Respiratory Diseases at the Central Hospital will find her.'

'Thank you,' said Jenna, going out and shutting the door.

On the way home from evening surgery, Jenna bought fish and chips again. That made the third time this week. It would have to stop. As well as playing havoc with her hips, it wouldn't do her professional reputation any good. In a little place like this, where everybody knew all about you, she'd better start practising what she preached. It was such a sweat, though, starting to cook so late, and she couldn't go to the Lobster Pot if Nick was likely to be there. He'd been so sure that cottage was to be their own private love nest and she'd had to make it clear that it wasn't.

Having parked the car, Jenna had her nightly battle to get the cottage door shut against the wind. She wondered if its owners had ever spent some time there in winter. She'd had to buy several electric fires. She switched on the oven and stuffed her fish supper in to keep hot while she loaded the washing machine. And the place could do with a dust as well. Jenna cursed the bad luck which had obliged her to quit the comfort of Harbour House.

Just as she was sitting down to supper at last, the phone rang. 'Please, not bloody Susan again,' she muttered. It seemed to her that Susan was hardly ever off the phone since she'd moved here. She'd changed her mind twice about the termination and was due to go in again tomorrow. If she refused a third time, it would be well nigh impossible to get the hospital to take her seriously.

Not Susan, but Meg with news of a daily who was simply bursting to come and do for Dr Jenna. 'Meg, you're a gem,' she breathed. 'I'm sitting here eating fish and chips to the tune of the washing machine and looking at the dust.'

Meg said that Mrs Mack would soon get everything to rights, not to mention being a dab hand at soup and pastry and such, and all Jenna had to do was leave her money on the kitchen table every Friday and remember to bring her spare keys with her tomorrow.

'Why can't everything be this simple?' she asked Meg next morning when, them having liked one another on sight, Mrs Mack went off with the keys in her hand, eager to get started.

Meg said that was the big question and how about this for a great big complication? Since she was clearly revving up for one of her gossips, Jenna said she'd love to hear all about it when she had a minute, but she didn't like the way the bloodstain on that patient's right foot was getting bigger every minute. 'I'll see him first, no matter what the others say,' she told Meg firmly.

Skipper Ferguson had managed to cut off his seaboot but his sock was thoroughly entangled in the pulpy mess that had been his foot. It was a miracle he hadn't bled to death while waiting stoically for surgery to start. Jenna roared for Meg to phone for an ambulance, then scrubbed up and tidied the foot as best she could, but what was needed was a lengthy session in Theatre, under a general anaesthetic. 'Hospital?' he said horrified. 'Is that not a bit over the top, Doctor?'

'You're a hardy lot, you fishermen,' Jenna said admiringly, 'but it's more than I can do to sort this. No, it's definitely hospital for you.'

'You fixed up Tam Walker with a plaster and let him back to sea, Doctor.'

'But he didn't have any broken bones and I'm afraid you have. Now there's nothing about anti-tetanus injections on your card——'

'That's because I've never had any, lass.'

Jenna remedied that, wrote a note detailing her treatment to the hospital casualty officer and helped him to hop along to the waiting-room.

With a start like that to the day, she was soon running late and dodged out through the house to begin her calls. There simply wasn't time to listen to Meg's latest titbit of gossip.

Jenna visited the sheltered housing complex first. The oldest inhabitant had gone wandering again and this time had been found in bed with her next door neighbour's husband. He was too deaf and short-sighted to realise the substitution until his wife brought it to his attention by bashing him over the head with the bedside lamp. How the interloper got in was a mystery, since the bed's rightful occupant insisted that she'd locked the door.

The warden's chief worry was not the old man's injury, but what her boss would say about security. Jenna suggested a midnight round to check and got on with stitching the patient's extensive scalp wound. Then she phoned the social work department and asked them to assess old Mrs Docherty for residential care before murder was done. 'And about time too,' said the warden. 'If you'd done that the first time, Doctor, none of this would have happened.'

Jenna had to agree, but pointed out how easy it was to say so with hindsight. 'I'll be gey glad when Dr William's up and about again,' was the woman's parting shot.

So will I, thought Jenna grimly, I could do with the odd five minutes to myself.

In order to minimise the risk of cross infection, Jenna had left her flu cases until last. By the time she'd finished, it was getting on for four and she was very hungry, having missed lunch yet again. She really must stop this. A doctor with a gastric ulcer was not the best advertisement for her own skill. She parked by the supermarket, determined to shop sensibly for a balanced meal. Rob was taking evening surgery, so barring emergencies she'd have plenty of time to cook tonight.

It was while she was deciding between chicken and lamb cutlets, that Jenna overheard two woman talking. 'Well, he was her boyfriend first,' said one.

Her friend murmured in disagreement.

'That's all very well,' said the first one, 'but if you ask me, she's had it coming. And as for the other two, they deserve each other. It's Dr Rob I'm sorry for.' Jenna pricked up her ears. 'It can't be very nice to find out that your girlfriend's been using you for a smoke-screen.' They moved on, still talking, and Jenna dodged along behind them not caring if anybody saw her.

'. . .all the ornaments off the mantelpiece—and

some of them gey valuable, according to Nora. Susan got a cut cheek from flying glass and the clock hit Dougal on the back of the head and nearly knocked him out. Nora says they looked like a pair of tinkers driving off, all bloody and battered. And the father's boiling up for a stroke, so—' But they had reached the check-out now and gossip was suspended.

Jenna had heard enough to set her thinking very hard. She'd quite forgotten why she was there and walked out empty-handed. Oblivious of curious glances from patients not used to being ignored in the street by the doctor, she hurried to her car, to try and make sense of that extraordinary conversation.

There was only one interpretation which fitted. Dougal—not Rob—was the father of Susan's child, hadn't minded as she'd thought he would and, when Shelagh found out, went berserk and started throwing things, the guilty pair had run away together. But this was guesswork. She had got to discover the truth, but how? And then came the terrible realisation that the dreadful, searing quarrel with Rob had all been for nothing. If she'd read those snippets of gossip aright, that was.

Meg! Could this be the complication she'd been bursting to reveal? Jenna switched on the engine in an agony of indecision, torn between her need to know the truth and dread at running into Rob whom she'd misjudged so horribly, to the point of destroying their relationship. I'll go home, she thought. Get myself together first. She couldn't though. It was as though the car had a homing instinct of its own, and was determined to return to its usual parking place.

Of course Meg wasn't there this early; Jenna had lost all track of time. She was standing in the passage, wondering what to do when the consulting room door opened and a patient came out. 'What are you doing here at this time?' Rob asked Jenna from the doorway.

'I came—to borrow a book!'

'Which one?' he asked.

'I——' She'd dried up completely, overcome again by the enormity of her misjudgement. She was convinced against all reason that he knew what she'd suspected and so there could be no end to his disgust.

'Well, go in and get it,' he said, frowning and nodding towards the patient walking deliberately slowly towards the waiting-room. His meaning was clear. For heaven's sake act normal, or the lord only knows what tales will be going the rounds tomorrow.

'Thank you, Doctor,' Jenna managed with supreme effort. 'I'll not be long.' Rob went to the dispensary and she dashed into the consulting room, snatching a book at random.

They met again in the doorway, dodging side to side in that mad sort of dance that hardly ever happened except in moments of tension and embarrassment. He stepped out of her way, after glancing at the spine of the book she was holding. 'Tropical diseases! What next?'

'I—I was reading something in a paper about—about bilharzia. And I thought I'd like to read up on it.'

'I'd have thought there was enough to do without bothering with something so unlikely. Unless of course, you're preparing for your next job.'

'My next job?' she echoed stupidly. The day's revelations had knocked every other thought out of her head.

'Or can he afford to keep you in idleness? Your lover,' he said savagely when she didn't answer. 'That paragon you're going back to.'

'Jake? To hell with Jake!' Jenna exploded, just as the telephone rang and the dull boom of the lifeboat alarm sounded simultaneously.

Jenna got to the phone first. 'Yes, yes—I understand. Sounds serious. I'm on my way.' Confused protesting at the other end of the line. 'How dare you?' she exploded again. 'I'm a doctor first and a woman second. You people——'

Rob snatched the phone from her grasp. 'Repeat that!' he ordered.

'You're not going—I am,' she yelled. 'I'm on call——' He had caught her in the crook of his arm and silenced her with his hand over her mouth. She wanted to bite him, but couldn't. Not Rob. . .

He'd put down the phone and was filling his case with instruments. 'Rob, please——'

'Take surgery!' he ordered, as he dashed out. Seconds later, she heard his car roaring away towards the lifeboat station. Jenna stood there, too weak with fear to move. She knew exactly what he faced. She should have gone. *She* was on call. And if she'd done well, she felt it would somehow have cancelled out her hideous misjudgement. She'd had no fear for her own safety, being too desperate and miserable to care. But Rob had gone into terrible danger and now she might never get the chance to tell him how much she loved him.

William had heard Rob's hasty departure and had linked it to the lifeboat alarm. When Jenna finally unfroze and crept through to the house, he was trying to get through to the station. 'Damn line's engaged,' he muttered, with an unaccustomed show of annoyance. Then he saw Jenna's tear-stained face. 'What you need is a good stiff drink,' he said.

'No—I'll be taking surgery. Rob's——' she swallowed pitifully. 'He's gone out with the lifeboat.'

'Do you know why?' His anxiety for his son was overriding his consideration for her.

'A fishing boat has gone aground on the Haggard rocks and one of the crew is trapped by the arm.'

William went ashen and dropped into a chair. 'Good God, he'll never manage to amputate in this!' As if in agreement, the gale lashed rain against the window and down the chimney, causing the fire to splutter. 'Even if they do get near enough to get a line across.'

'You mean, he'll have to be—be hauled across the sea? He could d-drown!' A sob caught in her throat. 'It should have been me! I'm the one on call.'

William got up and went to put his arms round her. 'My dear girl, you'd never have coped. You haven't the strength—no woman has. And that's not a sexist remark, it's the plain truth. Rob knew that. That's why he went.'

Jenna knew it too, deep down. 'I wish I were a man,' she sobbed against his chest.

'It's not all roses, Jenna—and in your case it would be a wicked waste,' he was saying when Mrs Cullen came in with the tea-tray. She eyed the tableau on the hearthrug curiously, but all she said was, 'I'll fetch another cup.'

When they were sitting side by side on the couch with plates of food they didn't want, William said by way of diverting her, 'I don't suppose you've heard the latest scandal.'

'To do with the MacArthur sisters?' He nodded. 'I overheard two women talking in the supermarket. It sounded as though they've fallen out.'

'That's one way of putting it,' said William. 'Susan is pregnant by Shelagh's husband and they've bolted.'

Now that the whole town knew, there couldn't be any harm in telling him. 'I knew about the baby. Susan consulted me over a month ago, but she wouldn't tell me who the father was. Just said she must have an abortion.'

William regarded her, his blue eyes knowing. 'I'm sure you wondered, though.'

She couldn't deny that. 'But it wasn't my business to—to pry. I advised her to tell him, but she said that was out of the question. So I arranged a hospital appointment, but she didn't follow through.'

'Oh, Jenna—how could you,' William said sadly and she knew he wasn't referring to her handling of Susan's problem.

Since it was useless to deny that too, she lifted her chin and asked, 'Isn't it usually the current boyfriend?'

He let that go. Perhaps he thought she'd had pain enough to be going on with. 'It looks as though Susan took your advice to involve the father after all—but whether it will all turn out for the best, I wouldn't like to say. What a mess!'

Jenna could only agree with that. 'It almost makes one want to head for the nearest nunnery,' she returned in a pathetic attempt at lightening the atmosphere. 'But first I must take evening surgery.'

'I could do it,' he offered. 'I don't suppose there'll be much of a turn-out in a storm like this.'

'Rob told me to do it. It was the last thing he said. . .'

William understood that too and said no more.

CHAPTER TEN

JENNA'S spirits sank to zero when she realised that her first patient of the session was Wilma Smith. But Wilma for once was almost cheerful, being full of the MacArthur scandal. 'Never mind them, how are you?' asked Jenna in an effort to get her off the subject.

'Oh, so-so. Isn't it dreadful the lengths some women will go to to get a man? I'd be ashamed!'

'As I don't know the background, I'd rather not comment,' said Jenna firmly. 'Is there anything specific you want to tell me, Miss Smith? Because if not—' She had sounded very determined and Wilma got the message.

But for once she had almost nothing to report. Her knee was better, the morning sickness forgotten and being on the bingo committee—Jenna didn't know there was such a thing—was taking a lot of her time. She even had to be reminded about her prescription for tranquillisers, having almost gone away without it.

A schoolboy with a simple ankle sprain next. Three minutes to apply a firm strapping. Another fierce gust that made the windows rattle. How could she concentrate when her mind was painting these horrific pictures of Rob, battling with the sea and the wind?

'I *said* when can I play again, Doctor?'

She gazed at the boy. 'Play what?'

He gazed back in youthful contempt. 'Football. That's how I did ma ankle. I *told* ye!'

Jenna rubbed her eyes as though to erase the horror. 'The strapping stays on for a week; longer if you're not pain-free. I'll decide. Then a light support while you increase activity gradually. No football for at least a month.'

'It's only a wee bit sprain.'

'That ankle has got to last you another seventy years. Take care of it.' Jenna buzzed for the next patient.

Another one obsessed with the latest scandal, like Wilma. She was very disappointed to see Jenna. 'I thocht Dr Rob was on the night.'

Jenna braced herself. 'Dr Rob is away with the lifeboat.'

'Is that so? Och, the puir man! 'Tis to be hoped he doesnae dae onnything desperate—and him that deceived.'

Jenna refused to be drawn. 'We've now got the reports on your back X-rays, Mrs Drever. There is some evidence of mild wear and tear, but nothing to worry about. It's something we all get as time goes by. The surgeon is arranging some physiotherapy for you and you'll be hearing from them shortly. Is the pain still keeping you awake at night?'

'Not since I got ma husband to put a board under my side o' the mattress like Dr Rob suggested. Was that another rocket goin' off then?'

'More like the joiner's boy on his motorbike. Well, if there's nothing more—' Jenna buzzed for the next patient.

She got a nasty look for that, but the patient left.

They all had their comments to make about the runaway lovers and Jenna was thankful that the storm had kept all but the hardiest at home.

'I'm away down to the lifeboat station to get the latest,' said Meg, when they had shut the door on the last patient. 'Are you coming with me, Doctor?'

'I can't leave Dr William on his own. Besides, there might be a call.'

'Aye, right enough. If I hear anything, I'll ring. There's a call box beside the fish market.'

William was sitting by the fire and staring into space. He brightened at the sight of Jenna. 'I suppose you're off now,' he said reluctantly.

'Only if you'd rather be on your own.'

'Don't be silly,' he said.

They sat side by side in silence for a while, each occupied with private, gloomy thoughts. When the phone rang, they both started. Jenna got to it first.

It was Meg phoning to say that there wasn't any news. 'But I'll keep you posted,' she promised.

'What about your mother?' asked Jenna.

'Let her get her own supper for a change. It'll do her good,' Meg answered.

When Jenna relayed that to William, he said it sounded as though the worm was turning and not before time.

They lapsed into silence again until called to supper which neither of them wanted, but pretended to enjoy.

At half past ten, Jenna tried to persuade William to go to bed. When he refused, she fetched blankets and a pillow and made him stretch out on the couch.

At eleven, Meg rang again to say that Rob and the injured fisherman had been lifted off the wreck by helicopter and the lifeboat was returning to port with the other members of the wrecked boat's crew. Jenna woke William to give him the good news. 'He did it, William. Rob got that man free.' Tears of relief were streaming down her cheeks.

'There were no fatalities, then?'

'Apparently not.'

'This time,' he sighed. 'The sea is a cruel master,

Jenna. I wonder how many folk remember that when they sit down to their fish suppers?'

'Not enough,' she said. 'I never did myself before I came to Port Lindsay.'

'I think you've learned to like Port Lindsay and its people,' William said carefully.

'Oh, I have—I have.'

'And they like you.' He paused. 'So it seems a pity that you're leaving us so soon.' His blue eyes were anxious and kind.

'I have to,' she whispered. 'You must see that.'

'Because you miss your former life and—your friends?'

Rob must have told him that. 'Because I don't deserve to stay,' she whispered, so low that it was doubtful if he heard. 'Cheer up, William,' she said more loudly. 'Third time lucky. There was a letter in this morning's mail from a very well qualified applicant for the locum post. If he could be persuaded to stay, think how that would raise the temperature around here,' she was saying as Mrs Cullen tapped on the door and looked in. 'There's a call for you, Dr Fielding. A patient.'

'Coming.' Jenna stood up and ran to the door, welcoming the interruption.

'I'm sorry we mean so little to you, Jenna,' she heard William say.

She turned to face him, her lower lip trembling pitifully. 'You don't,' she whispered. 'Quite the opposite. That's why I have to go.' Then fearing she'd said too much, she ran to the phone.

It wasn't really an emergency; just an anxious mother afraid that her child's flu symptoms might be meningitis. She apologised profusely as Jenna left. Jenna said, 'Not at all—you never know. You must never hesitate to call the doctor. Better safe than sorry.'

She emerged from that house into the teeth of the gale and only made it to the car by clinging to the garden railings. Should she go back to Harbour House or to the cottage? There was really no choice. She was the last person Rob would want to see when he came home exhausted.

The wind had dropped and both sea and sky were the same dark and angry grey when Jenna drove to work next morning. Rob was due to do surgery, but he'd be much too tired. She would do it. It was the least she could do.

Hearing footsteps in the passage, Jenna picked up the first card. 'Good morning, Mr Wilson,' she said with practised brightness as the door opened.

But it was Rob, not her first patient who came in. They stared at each other for a long moment. He looked drawn and tired and there was a large bruise on his forehead. Jenna was not to know that, but for the bruise, she looked much the same. Rob shut the door and leaned against it, watching her. 'This is kind of you,' he said at last, 'but there's no need. I'm quite able.'

She swallowed and said through stiff lips, 'I don't doubt your ability, I just thought you might be—I didn't even know you were back.'

'I got back about four—thanks to the RAF. They put me down on the football pitch.'

'It must have been—awful.' As she said it, she realised how inadequate it was as a comment.

'Let's just say I wouldn't want to repeat it.'

'Is the man all right? No, how can he be—I mean. . .'

'He's comfortable in hospital and he'll live. But a fisherman without a hand——'

'Quite. But at least he's alive, thanks to you.' Then, hardly knowing what she was saying, she went on, 'You were so right to go, Rob. I meant well, but I'd never have managed. A lifeboat is no place for a weak and feeble woman.'

'That was quite a speech,' he said with the ghost of a smile. 'Even if it wasn't entirely original. And thanks for staying with William. That was thoughtful.'

'I was glad of his company too.'

'You wouldn't have slept much anyway. Not in a storm like that.'

'It—took more than the storm to keep me awake,' she whispered.

'Yes, he said there was a call.'

Was he being deliberately obtuse? 'I was worried,' she said. 'I was—worried. . .' Her voice tailed off. She was remembering that quarrel and the bitterness of his contempt. Overcome by a tide of hopelessness, she looked down at the desk.

'William was still awake when I got home. We had—a very interesting talk,' said Rob, sounding a lot nearer now.

'He wanted to know all about the rescue,' she assumed, on the defensive.

'That too. He was really more concerned about—things nearer home.'

Jenna fiddled with a paper weight, dropping it with a clatter in her nervousness. 'He was kind enough to say I'd—I'd be missed if—that is, when I go. Or words to that effect.'

'Do you remember what your last words to me were before I dashed off last night?' he asked abruptly.

'I'm not sure. It was all so—so. . .'

'I was halfway to the station before I really took it in. You said "To hell with Jake".' She couldn't answer for the hope surging in her throat. 'Did you mean that?' he asked urgently.

'Oh, I meant it. I meant it,' she repeated under her breath.

'So all that stuff about going back to him. . .?'

'Was just so much hot air. Yes.'

'Then why did you say it?'

So he was going to make her spell it out, and who could blame him? Jenna raised her eyes at last. Gripping the edge of the desk she said falteringly, 'Susan had consulted me that afternoon. And when she didn't say who the father was, I jumped to the wrong conclusion. Silly, uncharitable—wrong of me, I know, but——'

'You'd been conditioned to expect men to behave badly,' he supplied.

She'd behaved abominably and didn't deserve to have excuses made for her. 'I don't know how you can be so forbearing,' she said fervently. 'I'd give ten years of my life to have all that dreadful stuff unsaid!'

Rob walked round the desk and reached for her hands. 'Ten years is far too much time to waste when we've wasted so much already,' he said softly.

'Rob, you don't mean—you can't! How can you when I've been so——?'

'Easily,' he said gently. 'I love you.'

'Oh, Rob——' Jenna did what she'd been longing to do ever since he walked through the door. She flung her arms round him and covered his face with kisses. 'Rob, darling Rob. You're so good—I don't deserve you, but I'll try. I love you too,' she said at last.

'I think I'd sort of gathered that,' he said unsteadily, 'but it's nice to have it confirmed.'

He barely had time to find her mouth before the phone rang. It was Meg. 'Look, I hate to interrupt,' she said, 'but the natives are getting restless.'

'Two minutes,' said Rob. He kissed Jenna gently on the lips. 'Would you think me horribly sexist if I insisted on taking this surgery, Doctor?'

'No, Doctor. Anything you say, Doctor. You're the boss.'

'Tamed at last,' he breathed, fitting in another warm embrace before pressing the buzzer.

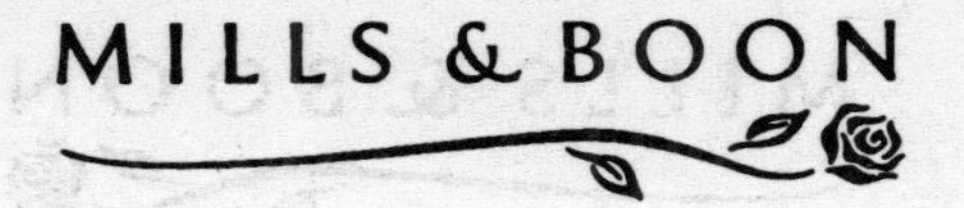

APRIL 1994 LARGE PRINT TITLES

Romance

A Heartless Marriage *Helen Brooks*	703	0 263 13765 1
Dawn Song *Sara Craven*	704	0 263 13766 X
Falling in Love *Charlotte Lamb*	705	0 263 13767 8
Flame of Love *Joanna Neil*	706	0 263 13768 6
Flight of Fantasy *Valerie Parv*	707	0 263 13769 4
Lady Be Mine *Catherine Spencer*	708	0 263 13770 8
West of Bohemia *Jessica Steele*	709	0 263 13771 6
Powerful Stranger *Patricia Wilson*	710	0 263 13772 4

LEGACY of LOVE

Heart of a Rose *Christine Franklin*	0 263 14004 0
The Cyprian's Sister *Paula Marshall*	0 263 14005 9

LOVE ON CALL

The Spice of Life *Caroline Anderson*	0 263 13982 4
Hearts in Hiding *Alice Grey*	0 263 13983 2

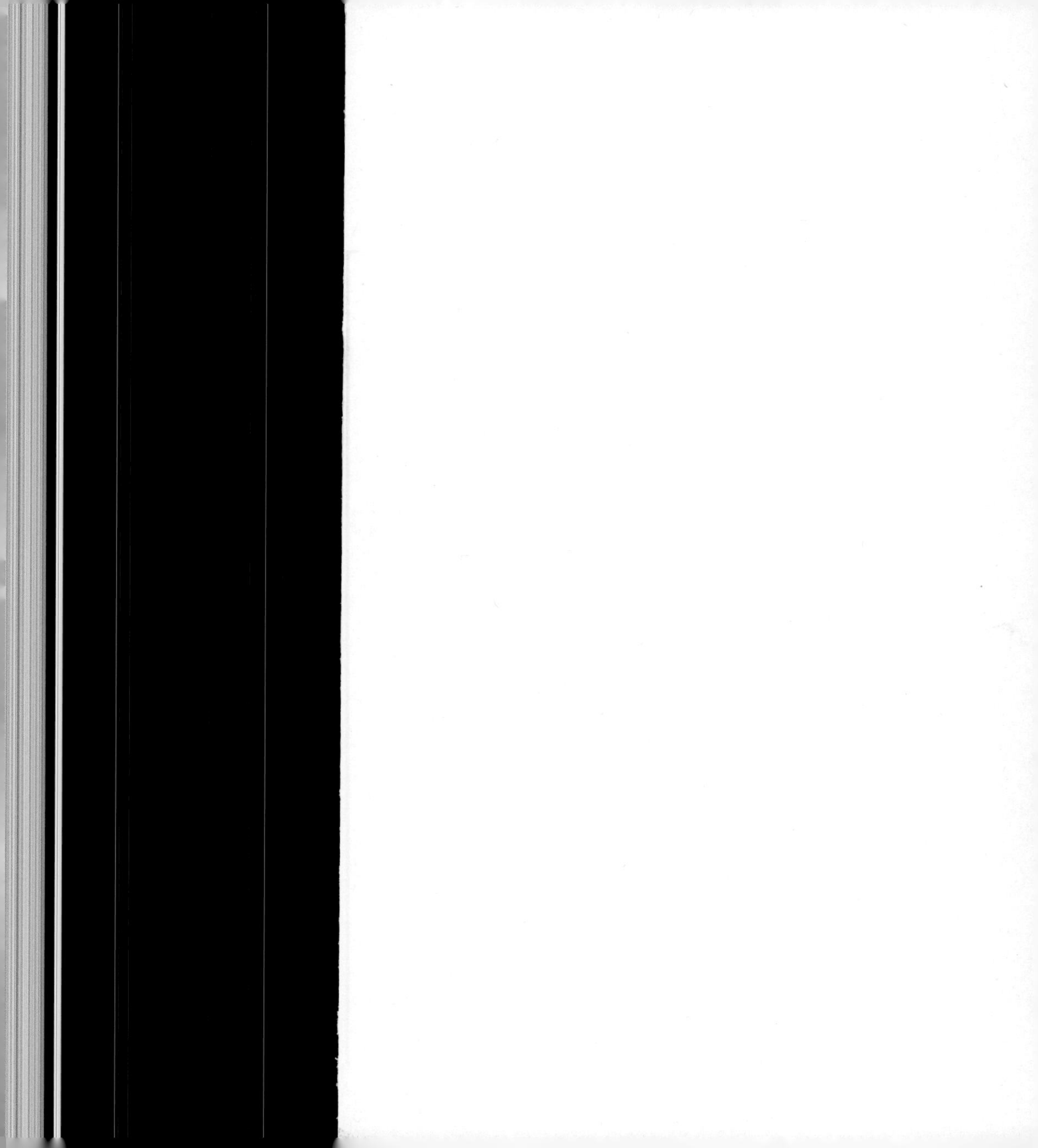